The Mysterious Lord Ballantine

Improper Ladies
Book One

THE LADIES WHO MISBEHAVE
AND THE GENTLEMEN WHO LOVE THEM.

MAGGI ANDERSEN

ARE YOU SIGNED UP FOR DRAGONBLADE'S BLOG?

You'll get the latest news and information on exclusive giveaways, exclusive excerpts, coming releases, sales, free books, cover reveals and more.

Check out our complete list of authors, too!

No spam, no junk. That's a promise!

Sign Up Here

www.dragonbladepublishing.com

Dearest Reader;

Thank you for your support of a small press. At Dragonblade Publishing, we strive to bring you the highest quality Historical Romance from some of the best authors in the business. Without your support, there is no 'us', so we sincerely hope you adore these stories and find some new favorite authors along the way.

Happy Reading!

CEO, Dragonblade Publishing

ADDITIONAL DRAGONBLADE BOOKS BY AUTHOR MAGGI ANDERSEN

Improper Ladies Series
The Mysterious Lord Ballantine (Book 1)

Improper Lords Series
The Duke's Masquerade (Book 1)
The Marquess Takes a Misstep (Book 2)
The Earl's Brazen Bargain (Book 3)

The Never Series
Never Doubt a Duke (Book 1)
Never Dance with a Marquess (Book 2)
Never Trust an Earl (Book 3)
Never Keep a Secret at Christmas (Novella)
Bella's Christmas Wish (Novella)
The Duke's Brown-Eyed Lady (Novella)

Dangerous Lords Series
The Baron's Betrothal (Book 1)
Seducing the Earl (Book 2)
The Viscount's Widowed Lady (Book 3)
Governess to the Duke's Heir (Book 4)
Eleanor Fitzherbert's Christmas Miracle (Novella)

Once a Wallflower Series
Presenting Miss Letitia (Book 1)
Introducing Miss Joanna (Book 2)
Announcing Miss Theodosia (Book 3)

The Lyon's Den Series
The Scandalous Lyon

Pirates of Britannia Series
Seduced by the Pirate

Also from Maggi Andersen
The Marquess Meets His Match (Novella)
Beth (Novella)
White Lady Lost (Novella)

Prologue

Ashburnham Hall, near Taunton, Somerset, Spring 1813

DIANA DESCENDED THE stairs, pulling on her riding gloves. She encountered her family's silver-haired butler in the great hall. "Good morning, Speirs. Has my father risen? He didn't come down to breakfast."

"Good morning, my lady. His Grace took breakfast in his studio." Speirs, always immaculately dressed and correct in all things, cleared his throat. "He has begun a new work."

Diana nodded, unsurprised by the information and unaffected by what she often found in the studio. Nothing her father did shocked her. But did this mean their trip to London might be delayed? Her ride forgotten, she hurried along the corridor.

She knocked at the door.

"Come!"

At the gruff reply, she entered her father's studio. The airy room was in the far corner of the east wing, where morning sunlight spilled in from the tall windows. Canvases stacked around the walls were in various stages of completion. The air was redolent of oil paint, turpentine, and linseed oil. A naked lady lay on a sofa, limbs partially entwined with a sheer fabric that hid little, her long, fair hair spread over the crimson, velvet upholstery. Papa was bent over his palette mixing the paint.

"Good morning, Papa." Diana turned away from the sight of so much pale flesh.

Her father scratched at his abundant silver locks with the handle of his paintbrush. His dark-blue eyes, a more mature version of her own, scowled at her. "Diana, you know better than to disturb me when I'm working."

"I beg your forgiveness, Papa. But I wondered if your plans for London have remained unchanged?" A new painting might keep her father here and put her promised trip to the metropolis for the Season on hold. "Shall I order my maid to pack?"

"Eh?" He stood before the easel where he'd sketched the faint outline of a naked lady, spreading thin, pale-blue paint onto the background. "I intend to finish this first. We will go next month. I must attend Prinny's affair. Impossible to ignore his dinner invitation again—he'll send his lackeys to annoy me. And he *has* bought two paintings of mine."

Despite her initial disappointment, Diana rallied. She was prepared to wait a month, assuming her father kept his word. She longed to visit the bustling metropolis again after being sent home in disgrace after her disastrous—in her father's estimation—two unsuccessful years on the marriage mart. And her plans for her future were only possible in London.

Papa looked over his shoulder, and his alert gaze focused on her. Her heart galloped. "I am determined to arrange a marriage this Season for you, my girl." He eyed her riding outfit but turned back to his canvas without comment. Diana breathed more easily. She could rely on his disinterest in women's fashions. "You're a good-looking miss with your mother's delicate features, and your breeding speaks for itself." He straightened, and after surveying his work, turned back to her. "I am still angry about Lord Amsberry informing me that his son flatly refused to wed you. And that after the marriage settlement was agreed upon and about to be signed." His forehead creased in a frown. "I don't know what you did to frighten away the young man, but it shall not happen again. I don't care how you conduct yourself after you're married. You can ride around naked if it pleases you and your husband. Married women can get away with a lot. But single women cannot draw too much attention to themselves. This coming Season, I expect you to dress elegantly with gowns provided by the best modistes I will pay for, and to behave in a manner that pleases a gentleman. So be warned."

"Yes, Papa," Diana said with false meekness. She trusted him to lose his focus on her once he launched this new painting. It would give her time to pick the man she wished to become her lover. And he would be nothing like the gentleman her father chose. He would be dashing, and handsome, and know how to please a lady.

When Lord Amsberry's son had visited her, it had been the first time she'd donned the men's riding clothes. She had met him at the stables, her pistol—one of the set of her father's dueling pistols she'd begun to carry for her safety—tucked into the waistband of her leather breeches. Her suitor had taken one look and blanched, then suddenly remembered an urgent appointment in Town.

It had been a test, and he had failed it.

Diana left the house and marched to the stables. The staff had grown accustomed to her odd choice of riding attire. And once having experienced the freedom of a man's clothing, she'd continued to wear them. She felt a good deal safer in them than when she was being hampered by the voluminous skirts of her habit. She thought she looked very smart with her black hat purchased from James Lock, her form-fitting black riding coat, and top boots, especially created for her by George Hoby. Not to mention the superbly comfortable brown leather breeches. Diana wished she could dress this way while riding in Hyde Park. She smiled to herself. That would have the biddies gawping and confirm their suspicions that she was her father's daughter. She'd heard the gossip. How many suitors had she spurned? Did she wish to marry? It didn't bother her much because her friends stood by her. And they were the ones who mattered.

Mounted on her roan mare, Artemis, Diana rode across the green meadows dotted with poppies and cornflowers. Warm grass and wildflowers scented the air. Pink dog roses bloomed in the hedgerows, and noisy, nesting birds gathered in the trees. She wished she could ride farther afield but kept within the estate boundary bordering the road, which led to all parts north, all the way to Scotland. How she would like to be journeying on that grand coach, drawn by four splendid thoroughbreds, which came toward her along the road.

Diana swiveled in the saddle at the thunder of horses' hooves coming fast from the south. The coachman had seen them, too. With a yell, he whipped up his horses, bringing the coach careering nearer to the boundary hedge, which, when she hunkered down, shielded Diana from view.

Within minutes, two masked highwaymen reached them and reined in beside the coach, their guns drawn. The coachman pulled the horses to a stop, while next to him, the groom dithered, scrambling for the rifle stowed at his feet.

To her knowledge, there had never been highway robbers in this vicinity. Pistol in hand, she took note of the earl's crest on the door panel, and, gathering her scattered wits, fired into the air.

The shot sounded deafening in the quiet countryside. The robbers yelled at each other and spun their horses around, staring into the scrub. When they failed to see where the shot had come from, they galloped their horses along the road to the north.

Diana backed Artemis up and jumped the hedge, drawing up beside the vehicle, tucking her dueling pistol back into her breeches, just as the coach door opened and a very tall, sleepy-eyed gentleman jumped onto the ground holding his pistol. "What the devil?" He stared at the groom and coachman on the box and thrust his hands through his rumpled, dark-brown hair, his heavy, dark eyebrows lowered. "That wasn't a hunter's shotgun I heard."

The groom climbed down. "Darndest thing, milord. We were about to be attacked by a pair of highwaymen and this here young, er"—he bent his head to indicate Diana—"woman scared them off."

The earl—at least she assumed it was he—swiveled and saw her where she'd backed Artemis into the shadows of leafy branches from a stately oak. She'd thought it wise to ride away before he saw her. But it was too late now. Alert, brown eyes took her in from her head to toe, then centered on the pistol tucked in at her waist. A slow grin deepened the lines, which bracketed his mouth as he bowed. "Beaufort, Earl of Ballantine. Then I must thank you, most profoundly, Miss...?"

He looked so wickedly masculine, she struggled to reply, unwilling to reveal her identity. "Diana, milord." She steadied Artemis, who sensed the change in her. "I was glad to be of service, as I can see it caught you unawares. Please continue your journey and I'll continue mine."

A smile tugged at his lips. "Don't hurry away. I'd like a word with you. If you'll give me a minute, Miss Diana." Cleared of any remnants of sleep, his dark-fringed, brown eyes were undoubtedly attractive. His lean face and square jaw, darkened by the shadow of a beard, and his sharply defined cheekbones, gave his face a rugged appeal. Diana took in his fine physique. A very attractive man. A man who, at least in appearance, would fit most women's dreams. But she also noted the manner with which he shoved the pistol into the back of his trousers and stood with feet planted apart, surveying the scene. Now, very much awake, he looked as if he expected trouble—and seemed well equipped to deal with it, should he find it. And she felt quite pleased to have dealt with it for him.

"Where did the rogues go, Will?" He turned back to his groom, who had jumped down and now shifted his feet, with his chin lowered.

"North, milord."

"It seems you have no more trouble on your hands," Diana said, hoping to leave, as Artemis raked the dirt with a hoof.

"Not immediately, at any rate. From where do you hail, Miss

Diana?"

His deep voice sent a tingle down her spine. Unnerved, she tightened her grip on the reins. "Over the way." Diana gestured with her head in a vague direction, eager to be gone. She was vulnerable here alone with this stranger. Not all lords could be trusted. Quite the opposite, she'd heard. "I'll be in trouble if I don't return this horse to her master, my lord." She turned Artemis's head and nudged her flank.

"So, like Diana, Goddess of the Hunt, you ride into my life and disappear again leaving me mystified?" he called after her. "I remain deep in your debt, Miss Diana, And hope we shall meet again."

Diana laughed as she steered her horse through the trees. She heard the earl instruct his coachman to continue on to Bath. Turning back, she watched the coach rattle away, the coachman cracking his whip over the dashing horses, the groom grimly clutching his gun.

She wondered if she would see the earl again when she and her father finally arrived in London. While it wouldn't be wise, after the way they had met, she couldn't help wishing she might.

Diana thought more about him as she rode home. Surely, he would attend some events during the Season. She'd never seen him before, but she'd remained at home in disgrace last year, after encouraging Lord Amsberry's heir to refuse her, and angering her father. She wasn't sorry. Not after his son had disappeared like a scared rabbit. Despite suffering months of interminable boredom as a result, it had been the right thing to do. Their natures would not have suited. She'd have made the poor man unhappy and herself as well. But Lord Ballantine! How different was he than the run-of-the-mill gentlemen she'd met. Who were those men who'd held up his coach? She suspected excitement would follow him wherever he went.

With a sigh, she urged Artemis into a canter, intent on arriving home before Papa noticed her missing and sent the groom after her. She must not risk his ire. Attending this coming Season had suddenly become even more interesting.

DAMIAN BEAUFORT III, Earl of Ballentine, glanced up at his groom on the box before boarding the coach. "Keep your gun at the ready and be quick to advise me if even some small thing doesn't look right." With his loaded pistol within reach of his hand beside him, he kept alert. Bloody hell, but his head hurt. It had been an exhausting three-day bacchanalian, with card play, too much imbibing and engaging women. It had made a perfect respite from the tension of his work, and he guessed he would see the benefits of it eventually, although not now, as he'd gotten precious little sleep. His thoughts returned to Miss Diana. No woman he'd met in Devon could match the fearless beauty who'd dressed in such unusual riding clothes and acted with such courage. It was regrettable that he hadn't been able to question the rogues. Could there have been another motive other than robbery behind the attack? Something to do with his spymaster? If so, this could mean trouble ahead.

The young woman had driven them off with a dueling pistol, no less. He chuckled and shook his head. Then he thought better of it when it threatened to fly off his shoulders. Beneath her wide-brimmed hat, she had scrutinized him, her unusual, dark-blue eyes the color of the ocean's deepest depths. He'd considered himself coolly appraised as he'd looked back at her. A curl of honey-gold-brown hair had teased her smooth cheek, her pink, full-lipped mouth as ripe as a plum. Riding astride in those breeches! With the longest and shapeliest legs he'd seen. Enough to give a man a cockstand. What the devil had she been doing gallivanting about in that garb, and with a pistol, no less? The daughter of the local squire, perhaps? She'd had to set about returning the horse, she'd said. He doubted it. Her clipped speech had given her away, and she'd been far too confident. That had been a gentleman's expensive dueling pistol and a devilishly fine thoroughbred she'd ridden with such ease. No squire would have trusted her with it. He knew they'd pulled up close to the Duke of Ashburnham's estate. He seemed to remember the duke had a daughter, although for the moment, her name escaped him. Wait, wasn't it Diana? Diana, Goddess of the Hunt, came to mind again, making him laugh. What would the Duke of Ashburnham make of his daughter riding about in men's clothes? Or was he too busy with his art? Rumor had it he had affairs with his models while painting their pictures. It must have worked well for him. His prized paintings fetched high prices at Sotheby's auctions.

Damian scratched his jaw where stubble itched. He'd left at first light and without his valet, had taken no time to shave. With a slow smile, a thought struck him. Might Miss Diana be one of Ashburnham's models? He laughed. Should it be so, he would keep an eye out for the painting. He'd buy it. Hang it on his drawing room wall. Sure to shock his infernal female relatives, who might think twice before arriving unannounced and pestering him. *Time you settled down. Come to dinner, I'd like you to meet Lady So-and-So...* Hadn't they heard the gossip? To keep hopeful mamas at bay, he had declared he wouldn't marry until his hair turned gray. Assuming he reached such a venerable age. He was still on the shady side of thirty, and there was much to do which could not include a wife and children.

But who is Diana? he mused, as her astonishing appearance, like a fierce Valkyrie, lingered in his mind's eye. The duke wasn't an acquaintance, so Damian couldn't ask him. But surely, a duke's unmarried daughter, if that was who she was, and he was now almost sure of it, would attend the Season, and he might see her there. By necessity, he must spend some time in London, after duty required him to visit an aunt in Bath. He groaned. He was fond of his Aunt Hattie, who had helped to raise him and his younger brother, Luke, after their mother had died young, but Hattie, true to form, was sure to have a lady in mind for him.

Damian gazed from the window at the road curving away

ahead of them, searching for any sign of a disturbance, a flock of unsettled birds, or rising dust, but there was only the bark of a fox, and the call of a crow, and then silence, broken by the rhythmic pounding of his carriage horses. His groom was young and too inexperienced to deal with masked gunmen. Damian hadn't considered it necessary to bring a footman this time and conceded that might prove a mistake. While the lady's dueling pistol had spooked the two men, it might not have been for long. Would they be game enough to try again? He was wide awake now and ready for them.

The more he thought about it, the more convinced he was that this had not been a chance meeting. It was not usual for highwaymen to rob coaches on this road. He suspected they'd been after not money, but him. If that were so, then who lay behind the attack? And what did they want, if not his death? Information? Their means of extracting it would not be pleasant and it made him angry he'd been so cavalier. His first stop when he finally reached London would be the Quartermaster General's Department at Army Headquarters in Horse Guards to consult his spymaster.

Chapter One

Daintith Park
Three weeks later

THE GUESTS, DRINKING wine, milled around the Marquess and Marchioness of Daintith's drawing room, speaking in subdued voices. When the news had come that her best friend, Lady Anne, had been kidnapped while returning from a shopping trip in Bath, Diana had wept until her pillow had been soaked. No trace of her had been found, even after her father had paid a ransom. Now, Diana had no more tears to shed, and a lump blocked her dry throat.

Anne's ill mother absent, Lord Daintith walked among the guests looking strained. Anne had admitted privately to Diana to struggling to like her father, whom she found overbearing, but perhaps he loved his daughter.

"The gentleman in black in the corner is Viscount Withnell," Grandmama whispered. "Apparently, his and Anne's betrothal was about to be announced when she was taken."

Diana saw no sign that the viscount was heartbroken. He looked impatient, tapping his hand against his thigh, as if he wished to leave. He was a tall man with a hard mouth. But grief affected people differently, she reminded herself.

The last letter Anne had written to her mentioned a gentleman her father had been considering for her husband. This, apparently, was he.

With a nod to her sorrowful grandmother, who stood with her father, Diana slipped out through the open French doors onto the terrace. Everyone talked as if Anne were gone forever. They could not give up on her. They must not. Surely, it was possible to uncover something that might lead them to the place where Anne was held? Diana could not believe she was dead. She wasn't prepared to believe it.

Anne's maid had been sent home carrying a note from the kidnappers with instructions for where to leave the ransom. She had become hysterical and had been sent off to stay with her mother.

Though the weeks since Anne's disappearance had blurred together, Diana remembered, a few days after she'd gotten the news, riding her horse to the Daintith estate. Instead of heading to the front door, as she always had, she'd gone to the stables. She'd found Joseph Cullin, the groom who'd been in attendance to Anne's carriage that day, grooming a horse on the cobbles.

He swung around as she entered the courtyard, his jaw agape. "Lady Diana!"

Diana dismounted from Artemis. "A sad day, Joseph. Can you tell me how it happened?"

"I told them everything I know, my lady," he said, his voice trembling.

"Yes, but, Joseph, I need to know."

He sniffed and wiped his nose on his sleeve. "The masked man came riding out of the trees, Lady Diana. He fired his gun into the air..." Joseph paused, his pale face gone paler. "Bullen pulled up the horses. Then the rogue rode over and pulled open the carriage door. He demanded Lady Anne come with him. The maid screamed, and our lady tried to calm her.

"Before we knew what was what, he'd pulled Lady Anne from the carriage, and atop his horse. She looked about to faint as he rode off into the trees with her. Her little dog, Toby, leapt down from the coach and

chased after them. Haven't seen hide nor hair of either of them since."

Diana's stomach twisted and she felt sick. "What did this villain look like?"

"He was big, wore an old coat and breeches, his hat pulled low. A red handkerchief tied over his lower face muffled his voice." Joseph dragged in a breath. "I'll never forget his eyes. He made me freeze with fear, my lady," he confessed, looking at his boots.

"It must have been very frightening, Joseph. Whereabouts did it happen?"

The groom gazed around at the stables. "I can't tell you no more, my lady. Not proper for you to be here. It's more than my job's worth to speak of it. Old Bullen has got it in for me as it is." He turned away and led the horse into the stables.

Diana, shocked, tears blinding her, could do nothing but ride home again.

Leaving the mourners in the drawing room, Diana stepped down from the terrace and walked along the drive to the stables. Their coachman, John Bullen, groaned. "I still can't believe it," he said with an audible gulp. "We was unprepared for such an attack. Joseph, the groom, feared he'd be blamed, because he hadn't reached for his gun. He felt sure the master would let him go without a character. So, he's run off." He shook his head. "They say Lady Daintith has taken sick. Such a sweet lady was Lady Anne. Always with a smile for me when I brought the coach around. This family will never be the same again."

"Where was the ransom left?" Diana asked him.

Bullen shrugged. "No idea, my lady. Apparently, Lord Daintith was told to come alone. He went off in his curricle."

"Was he gone long?" Diana asked, wondering where he had gone.

"He returned that evening. Didn't say a word to us. The horses were in a sweat, so he'd driven them hard."

"Where was the coach held up?"

"On the woodland road, only a few miles from here."

Diana bit the inside of her cheek to quell her own rising panic as she returned to the house. How she might learn more? Was it even possible to search for Anne herself? She must try. She'd make a plan.

In the coach returning home with her father and grandmother, Diana dared to ask more. "Papa, was the ransom collected?"

"It was."

"Did Lord Daintith tell you where he left the ransom? Was he met by someone?"

Her father studied her. "Not to my knowledge. Why do you ask, Diana?"

She tried to sound calm. "I'm curious."

"An inn," her father said reluctantly. "The Hare and Hounds."

"Where is the inn?"

"I've no idea," Papa said. "Somewhere disreputable, I am sure. Best we put this behind us, Diana. Shall we move on to more pleasing topics?" He sighed heavily, his face grim. "I wouldn't like to see you spoil your Season in London. A thorough search was made by Bow Street. Nothing can bring Lady Anne back." He frowned. "You should take note, Diana. How dangerous the world is for an unprotected woman. Never ride without a groom."

Diana firmed her lips to keep from mentioning Anne had not been alone. She had traveled with a trusted staff.

Grandmama squeezed Diana's arm in sympathy, and the rest of the journey passed in silence, while Diana thirsting for more knowledge, fought not to argue with him, and rage against his callous comments, knowing it would do no good.

London
Four weeks later

ALTHOUGH DIANA NOW had little desire to be in London, ten days later, at her father's urging, she'd accompanied him to their Mayfair home for the Season.

They had been in the city for three weeks and as Diana was still deeply distressed, after learning that Anne's mother had died of a broken heart shortly after the memorial for Anne, she found dancing with gentlemen dull and struggled to focus. This all seemed like a waste of her time when she could be out searching for Anne.

Papa had insisted on a new wardrobe for her, which required many tedious fittings and shopping trips, which had made Grandmama complain her feet hurt. The clothes were beautiful, and Diana knew she was ungrateful, but she couldn't make herself care.

Her father behaved in an extremely vexing fashion. Usually, this many weeks after their arrival in London, he would have lost interest in her, but this year, he seemed very determined. While he tolerated her, she had no illusions that he cared deeply for her. He'd wished for a son and heir, and Mama, whose health had always been fragile, could not give him one.

Diana only hoped when Papa's latest painting caused the usual fuss in a gallery on Bond Street, it would wholly capture his attention, as it had on previous occasions.

Through discreet inquiries, she'd discovered that the Earl of Ballantine had a reputation for avoiding marriage. The news pleased her. He appeared to fit the part of an exciting lover splendidly. But despite Diana attending all the social events in the past weeks with her grandmama, he'd failed to appear at any of them. How long could she hold off her father before he insisted she agree to marry one of those gentlemen he had in mind for her?

Tonight at the Foresters' ball, Diana wore a white net ballgown with pink silk roses at the hem and on the train she thought suited her, and she approved of the soft-white feathers and diamond comb in her hair. Papa, clearly determined to see her wed, had removed the ruby-and-diamond pendant from the family's parure, kept at the bank, for her to wear. It nestled coolly against her cleavage in the low-necked gown. She thought the overall effect a cut above the demure, white muslin she'd worn in the past. Diana disliked dressing like every other young woman, and at twenty-one she considered herself old enough to dress how she liked. Fortunately, Papa didn't care, and Grandmama was rather unconventional herself with a very interesting past Diana hoped someday to hear more about.

A finger through the loop to hold up her train, she performed the cotillion, partnered by her father's friend, the diplomat Sir Charles Stuart. While the dance separated them, her gaze drifted over the sparkling, perfumed crowd, moving about the rim of the dance floor. Then she spotted him. *Lord Ballantine.* His graceful, relaxed stance, with one leg slightly thrust forward, caught her eye as he stood among a group of distinguished gentlemen. She craned her neck as she danced past, recognizing the prime minister, Lord Liverpool, a serious, composed gentleman, and the fair-haired foreign minister, Lord Castlereagh, among them. Sir George Scovell appeared to hold sway, and they all listened to the round-faced, balding gentleman intently. The news from the war was in the forefront of most people's minds, although it seldom reached the newspapers for days and sometimes longer.

The steps brought Diana's dance partner back to her side. She liked Sir Charles, who was attractive and had the exquisite manners of a diplomat. She smiled warmly, a little guilty for being so inattentive.

His eyes twinkled. "When you smile, Lady Diana, I sense all the gentlemen in the ballroom long to bask in it. A few suitors among them, perhaps?"

"No doubt my father has his eye on those."

"You don't appear keen for marriage, my lady."

"I wish not to be rushed, Sir Charles. But my father thinks differently."

"Ah. Such is often the case." He laughed. "Have pity. I imagine it would be difficult to be the father of a lovely, young woman."

He didn't add *without a mother to guide her*. But she had to admit he was right. She'd never considered her father's position, so intent was she on her own.

As the dance drew them apart again, Diana wondered who among her acquaintances might properly introduce her to Lord Ballantine. She glanced speculatively at the man leading her through the steps. Sir Charles Stuart would be sure to know him. Could she be so bold as to ask him? She was confident he would agree, but then she dismissed the idea when she realized her father would hear of it.

Was an introduction necessary? They had met, although not the way her father would have approved of, and from where Papa stood surrounded by friends, he still observed her. She had to be careful. Perhaps she could rely on Ballantine to approach her, although so far, he'd made no attempt to even acknowledge her. Perhaps he'd failed to recognize her? She wasn't sure how she felt about that but continued to glance at him when the steps of the dance brought him into view.

His manner seemed dissimilar to the rake a friend had pointed out to her. She remembered that man's restless eyes following the prettiest women. Was she mistaken in what she'd seen in Ballantine during their brief meeting? He was quite different from the gentlemen she'd met, all of whom seemed so aware of their importance and their place in society. When he left the group, he remained a little aloof from those who crowded around him and sought his patronage. She watched him smile and offer a brief word time and again, before moving on. Unlike her father. Papa appeared to relish the attention of toad-eaters. But then it gave him a chance to talk about his art.

She really must learn more about Lord Ballantine.

As she danced, her mother, gone these last six years, was never far from her mind. She had loved Mama dearly and missed her warmth and loving support. *"Marry only for love, Diana,"* she would say, urging Diana to grasp life with both hands. But she'd fallen ill when Diana had been sixteen and had failed to see her enter society.

Her mother had wished to be an opera singer, but Grandpapa had refused, insisting she marry. Mama had performed in London drawing rooms and at musical evenings after Diana's birth, and she'd been received with great applause. The memory of her singing in her glorious voice made Diana proud and sad. Had her parents ever loved each other? They had always been polite, but she'd seen no sign of genuine affection between them as she'd grown up. Her father's behavior must have humiliated her mother. Such thoughts brought tears to her eyes. She hastily blinked them away, afraid she would embarrass herself, as the dance concluded.

Returning to her seat, Diana took a deep breath. Her mother would have been proud of her, however she chose to live her life, and Diana would not go meekly into an arranged marriage, knowing it would stultify her. When Diana had told Anne about her plan to take a lover before marriage, Anne had been shocked. She'd observed proprieties, and in that way, she and Diana differed. *"Never draw too much attention to yourself by your behavior,"* Diana remembered Anne saying.

But what bitter irony when Anne had been plucked from the supposed safety of her carriage and no one had seen her since. Diana drew in a sharp breath, putting a hand to her chest. Her dearest friend had been suffering for weeks and could be hurt or dead, while here she was at a ball enjoying frivolity. But she couldn't make herself believe Anne was dead. If only she were able to go in search of her. Impossible to do it alone. Her father would find her and bring her back, and then where would she be? Watched even more closely? She must find a man who would help her. Pulled down with grief and a sense of hopelessness, she knew how difficult it would be to achieve. She swallowed the lump in her throat. Life could be so cruel.

What had happened to Anne only firmed Diana's belief that one should grasp life with both hands. She still held out hope that she might find a suitable man to become her lover, who would subsequently aid her in her search.

She glanced back at Lord Ballantine. She doubted he'd be a good husband, but he would be an exciting lover. Her heart thumped just to look at his tall, elegantly clad body and speculate about how he looked without clothes. Such thoughts brought a blush to her cheeks.

Ballantine turned her way. It was difficult in the smoky air to be sure if he looked at her, but a prickle of awareness made her rub her nape. Did he recognize her? If so, he now knew who she was. But was he a rake? It had been her decision not to pick one for a lover. Rakes only had to crook their little finger, and women followed. And it wasn't in her nature to dance to any man's tune. They were not admirable people in anyone's estimation, as they seldom remained loyal to one lady. And were known to ruin naïve, young debutantes. Well, she didn't consider herself naïve. Could she take a chance on Ballantine, should the opportunity present itself? But should they become lovers, she must be careful not to care too much or let him hurt her.

AFTER THE ATTACK on Damian's coach had raised some red flags, Sir George Scovell, Damian's spymaster, had sent him to lie low in Lisbon. Damian had only recently returned. There was a French spy ring somewhere in London, and it was possible that Damian's cover had been blown.

It had been a successful trip. Damian had brought back important information for Scovell, who was an outstanding code breaker, to decrypt. The Foresters' ball was Damian's first engagement since his return. After two documents containing vital information intended to be sent to Arthur Wellesley Marquess of Wellington, had been stolen, Damian had been called back into action in London. His mission: to find the spies behind the theft and retrieve the documents. If they had not left the country and fallen into the wrong hands. A spate of storms over the Channel prevented smaller vessels from setting sail, and that may have delayed them.

People avidly discussed the news from Spain. Arthur Wellesley's troops had crossed the Bidasoa River in the north of Spain and an enemy force occupied French soil for the first time in twenty years.

Damian had grown profoundly tired of the war. He hated to see the despair and poverty here in London and around the country, caused by long years of fighting the French. In London, he had spoken to emotionally scarred and maimed soldiers, their futures uncertain, and wished he had the means to help them.

Watching the dancers, he admitted to being ready for a light-hearted dalliance. A charming lady to while away the hours until his next assignment sent him beyond English shores again.

With a final flourish, the musicians lowered their instruments and the heated dancers promenaded from the floor, seeking refreshment. A young woman on Sir Charles Stuart's arm glanced his way. She smiled, but he noticed sadness in her eyes. Their gazes caught, and for a startling moment, held.

Dash it all, it was the lady who had been constantly in his thoughts since their meeting when the highwaymen had attacked his coach. Damian bowed to the men in his company. "Please excuse me, gentlemen."

"Ballantine has spied his next conquest," a fellow said behind him, followed by group laughter.

Damian turned with a wink. "Give me time, gentlemen."

"An hour, at least." Castlereagh laughed.

"Who is the lady?" Scovell asked, a glimmer of a smile in his intelligent, blue eyes.

"I have yet to learn her full name," Damian said, unwilling to reveal more. "She has escaped me thus far."

Heads shook disbelievingly. "What a sorry tale," Liverpool observed with a grin. "Let us hope your fickle reputation with the ladies does not precede you."

With a chuckle, Damian left them. Wellesley's right-hand man, the diplomat Sir Charles Stuart, led the tall, slim young woman over to the sofa, where an older lady sat waiting. Damian crossed the floor for a closer view of Miss Diana. The young woman, who remarkably had scared away the robbers with her dueling pistol. Miss Diana. She was no squire's daughter. If she'd been fetching in breeches, tonight, she was beautiful in the delicate net gown, the candlelight picking out golden streaks in her honey-brown hair. Unlike most debutantes, who seemed to favor dainty, gold jewelry and pearls to complement the pale gowns they wore these days, a fine diamond-and-emerald jewel nestled against her milky skin in the low-cut gown. But Miss Diana—if that was her correct title—was unlike most debutantes and cast even the prettiest of them into the shade.

Needing to be sure his suspicions were correct, Damian followed her dance partner, Sir Charles, as he threaded his way through the crowd. On reaching him, Damian tapped him on the shoulder. "Charles, the lady with whom you just partnered for the cotillion. Her name?"

Charles cocked an amused eyebrow. "Lady Diana Stafford, the Duke of Ashburnham's daughter."

Damian nodded. So he had been right. As extraordinary as it might have been, the lady in men's breeches brandishing a dueling pistol had been the duke's daughter.

"She's a pretty woman, but beware, Ashburnham is determined to see her engaged this year and is on the lookout for the right man," Charles said, a twinkle of mischief in his eyes. "Since he is unlikely to have been informed about your covert activities, he might view you favorably."

"I shan't give him a reason to consider me. But I confess to being surprised Lady Diana hasn't married."

Charles smiled. "She appears averse to the idea of matrimony. The Staffords are a rare breed. They care little for society's doctrines. But tread carefully. Your dangerous work for Scovell places you in a similar position as me. A wife would make you vulnerable. When you become worried and distracted by loved ones left at home, you can make dangerous mistakes. I shall not consider marriage until the war is over."

Damian nodded. Lady Diana was unusual and utterly fascinating. But marriage was not on his mind. "Thanks for the warning, Charles." He had been about to ask him to introduce him to Lady Diana but considered it unwise.

"Best avoid her, lest she draw you in." Charles laughed. "She is the lady to do so."

While Damian silently agreed, the temptation to know more about her still tugged at him. It was his nature to sail close to the wind. His father had been a cautious, conservative man who'd warned Damian to be careful. *"Never ride in the rain and subject yourself to a lung complaint." "Never take a horse over a high jump, or you might break your neck." "Never venture into those parts of London where it is unsafe. You risk contracting a disease that could carry you off."*

But his younger sister, Mary, had died at eight years old, after she'd fallen from a pony, having sneaked out to ride it behind their father's back. Without the aid of a groom, she'd tried to take the pony over a fence. He and Luke had been heartbroken. Father had carried on in that stiff-upper-lip fashion expected of aristocrats, but he'd sickened and died before he'd turned forty-five, having seldom ventured farther than his estate. In Damian's opinion, life was precarious whatever one chose to do. Their premature deaths had made him determined not to live as his father had, letting life slip by while he worried about what might carry him off.

Damian found himself attracted to Lady Diana's unaffected honesty. She hadn't flirted with him like other women, although he sensed there was something beneath her bravado. The shadow in her eyes made him suspect she'd been badly hurt, and it drew him to her. But he wasn't a fool. He was cautious—had to be in his line of work, which he had no intention of giving up until

England won the war. As his gaze rested on her, remembering her riding astride with those long legs, he weighed up the intriguing possibility of discovering if she would be as passionate and as vitally alive as he suspected, against landing himself deep in hot water. And not to be dismissed was Scovell's order to unearth the French spy ring still operating somewhere in London.

Lady Diana talked to their hostess, Lady Forester. A word in that lady's ear, and Damian and Lady Diana would dance before the night was over. Dash it all, why not? He took steps toward where she chatted to her hostess, then stopped. What was he doing? A duke's daughter. No matter if she was everything he hoped for, he could not bed her. Her father would have him banished to the New Hebrides. And Damian wouldn't want her reputation to suffer.

Before he could retreat, Lady Forester, smiling, advanced toward him over the ballroom floor, with Lady Diana's arm tucked into hers. Lady Diana must have requested it. His eager response brought a soft moan to his lips.

Chapter Two

WHEN LORD BALLANTINE led Diana onto the dance floor for the waltz, she noticed the pause in conversation among the ladies who sat watching them. She glanced up at his attractive profile. Did they make more of it than there was? He didn't flirt with her, and he had actually said little beyond the usual pleasantries, even after Lady Forester had left them and they were alone on the dance floor.

Her hand rested on his forearm, and even through her gloves and his silk coat, she felt a steely strength in him.

As the musicians took up their instruments, Diana's confidence in her ability to take Ballantine as her lover wavered slightly. His big hand was in hers, and the other warm at her waist. He seemed so large, and so male. He was so unlike the pampered gentlemen who usually partnered with her at balls. The spoiled sons of lords whose sense of superiority and confidence came from their wealth and birth. Ballantine seemed different. It was as if he had personally faced danger and been tested to the utmost. It wouldn't surprise her to learn he'd been a soldier. There was always something gritty and resolute about men who fought for their country. But surely, if that were the case, he would still have been fighting in Spain, not here dancing with her. A small sigh escaped. How handsome he would look in uniform. She tried to calm herself before he realized she was nervous, and wondered at it. She was behaving like a goose over a man. Like all flirtatious women whose behavior she had initially frowned upon but now understood. *Keep your head!* Diana frowned. But might it be her heart that was in danger?

Ballantine's mouth quirked, and a wicked sparkle lit his brown eyes.

"A penny for your thoughts, Lady Diana?"

Diana struggled to come up with a witty reply and, in the end, shrugged. "Nothing of interest, my lord. I heard the Prince of Wales might come tonight." It was an outright lie, but he'd caught her off guard and she could think of nothing else.

"You are eager to see His Highness?"

She nodded. "Isn't everyone?" Actually, she disliked the prince, and for many reasons, not least how ridiculously extravagant he was wasting money when the long war had brought such poverty to England.

"I am pleased to have this opportunity to thank you again for your brave intervention when masked gunmen attacked my coach." He smiled into her eyes. "It could have been very dangerous for you. They might have followed you."

"Onto my father's land? I think not. I hid myself well, and by firing my gun, I gave you and your groom time to draw your weapons." She cast him a level glance, admitting he would have handled the situation well without her help. "I acted on instinct. I hadn't seen you when I fired my gun. You had no more trouble after you continued your journey?"

"No. They made no further attempt." He smiled. "If they'd known a lady had scared them away, it would have been a different story, would it not? Do you often carry a pistol?"

Did he find her amusing? She detected no sign of it. In fact, she thought he looked concerned. A woman with a gun? Heavens above! Such a danger to herself and others! Anne was an example of what happened to women who were defenseless, she thought sadly. It made her determined to be prepared should anything untoward present itself. "I believe it's wise, as I ride alone," she said more sharply than she'd intended.

He raised his eyebrows. "While on your father's estate?"

"Yes. Even then. A good friend, Lady Anne Daintith, was abducted for ransom, two miles from her home." Despite her efforts to sound calm, her voice shook.

"I heard about that," he said gently. "I'm sorry. She was your friend. A dreadful business."

At the compassionate note in his voice, Diana's shoulders tensed. She dragged in a breath. The tragedy occurred nearly two months ago, and losing Anne in such a cruel way was still raw. Bitterness and anger tightened her throat, making her voice tremble. "Men held up Anne's carriage. They abducted her," she said, swallowing.

It made her angry to think her father would continue to force the marriage issue when her friend could be dead.

The soft expression in his eyes made her afraid she might cry. She bit her lip hard, unwilling for him to know how distressed she was. *I need a distraction*, she thought desperately. *At least until I can find a way to go in search of Anne. Would a passionate affair serve? What if I died in the attempt to find her? Without ever having experienced passion?*

"You have only one chance to hit someone with a dueling pistol," he said. "I trust you are a good shot?"

"I am." Startled by his question, she gained some modicum of composure, relieved the conversation had shifted onto surer ground. After Anne's disappearance, she'd practiced endlessly firing at pumpkins atop a wall on her father's estate.

"Somehow, I am not surprised. Although…" He paused. "It is one of the few things about you, Lady Diana, thus far that doesn't surprise me."

She raised questioning eyebrows, not sure she wanted to hear his reasons. But curiosity got the better of her. "I'm not sure what you mean, sir."

"Only that you seem to be of a very determined nature. You don't like to be told what to do, nor do you feel the need to emulate others." He cocked an eyebrow. "Am I right?"

He was astute in his assessment of her character, but she'd never admit it. She raised a shoulder. "My grandmother says I am uncommonly outspoken." Most men wanted women to be obedient and meek. Perhaps he did too. Well, she wasn't, and she would never be.

"If you must carry a gun," he said, interrupting her rancorous thoughts, "I would prefer you were better armed." His deep voice made the observation sound so...*sensual*. His warm, brown eyes flickered down to where her sharp intake of breath had raised her breasts, much of which were revealed in the scoop-necked gown. "A dueling pistol is an inadequate weapon to defend yourself."

"That probably is good advice, but impractical, alas."

"I don't see why."

Unlike other men, he appeared to look at her as if he were really interested in her, and not blinded by the ambition to marry a duke's daughter, or the handsome dowry her father had placed on her.

"It's impossible for me to buy a pistol, although you might assist me," she said as her heart raced. *Heavens!* She felt as if she were spinning out of her depth. But she mustn't let a chance like this pass her by. Lord Ballantine could satisfy her curiosity about experiencing true passion. If he became her lover, would he agree to help her carry out her plan to find Anne? She had given the matter a lot of thought. How she would tell her father she was invited to stay with her friend, Penny, in Bath. Papa would agree, as she'd stayed with Penny's family before. There were a few details to be worked out, but making her plan a reality had, she realized now, all hinged on seeing Lord Ballantine again.

Ballantine's lip quirked. "Your father would be rightly angry should I get a gun for you, and you would still require lessons to manage it. I can't say I've seen a woman at Manton's buying a pistol or firing at wafers in the shooting gallery."

"Papa wouldn't care," she said airily. "He allows me a great deal of latitude."

"As I have seen," he said, the grooves on each side of his well-formed lips deepening. "But this might be going a little too far."

He wasn't dismissing it out of hand. Could she persuade him to help her? He was right. The dueling pistol was heavy and awkward. It would not suit her purpose. "Please, can't I prevail upon you to purchase one for me? A small pistol to fit in my reticule?"

"No, Lady Diana. I will not."

She dropped her chin, deeply disappointed.

"Come, don't you see what a difficult position that would place me in?" He bent slightly to gaze into her eyes. "What would your father make of that?"

How they'd first met hovered between them, silencing them for a few moments. She needed that pistol, but it wasn't the right time to tell him the reason, although her frustration deepened with every day that passed. "Well, if you are afraid of my father…" she said with an annoyed shrug.

He laughed. "You think me ungrateful. I assure you I am grateful, for waking me so nicely and sending the highwaymen riding for their lives before I had to a chance to even gather my wits about me."

He was making fun of her, but she couldn't help a grin.

The music began, and a large, warm hand spanned the back of her waist as the dance commenced. Her heart thumped with the rising tempo of Mozart's waltz music. She breathed in his fresh scent, starch and a musky soap, and something essentially male. Very much aware of their closeness, she darted a glance at his face, until he turned her. Spinning and coming together left her breathless to do anything but mind her steps. He was an excellent dancer, moving her gracefully around the dance floor as other couples twirled by. She glanced up at the hard line of his jaw. Did he really mean to refuse to help her? She hadn't given up on Lord Ballantine yet. He was right. It wasn't in her nature, not until she absolutely had to admit defeat.

"YOUR CHEEKS ARE delightfully pink, Lady Diana," Damian said. "Shall I slow the pace?"

Lady Diana's expression gently mocked him. "You make me sound like a dowager. I love to dance. And to gallop my horse over the meadows at home."

Damian swept her over the floor, turning her, then reversing. He enjoyed making her gasp. Dancing was akin to bedding a woman in his estimation, although only the first step in a seduction. Such thoughts led to how delicious it would be to have her moaning with pleasure beneath him. A pleasure he would never have, sadly.

Their steps slowed with the music, and she laughed, clutching his shoulder. It pleased him to see her so happy, if only for a moment. The horror of losing her friend had obviously affected her a good deal. It must have been hard for her to accept her friend was dead, but from his experience of such crimes, they almost always ended badly.

The music rose again, sending them twirling, then having reached its crescendo, slowed and then the dance ended.

A loud murmur rose as the dancers caught their breaths.

With a gasp, Lady Diana held on to his arm. "You are an accomplished dancer, my lord."

His gaze roamed appreciatively over her graceful body and back to her delicately featured face, her firmly rounded chin, her heavy mane of gold-brown hair that invited a man's hands. Oh, to see it down around her bare shoulders. She was enchanting. He must see her again. "Might I find you riding in Hyde Park tomorrow?"

"You might. I usually ride at nine o'clock before the rush."

"So early? You shall not be abed until dawn," he observed.

"I can never sleep late in the city. The mornings here are so noisy."

Or she's too troubled by her friend's disappearance to sleep well, perhaps. "Then I hope to see you in Rotten Row on Saturday morning."

It wasn't his inclination to ride often while in London—it was inferior to the country—but for her, he certainly would. He offered her his arm to escort her from the floor.

"I shall look forward to seeing you should you be there, my lord."

After leaving her with the dowager duchess, who looked him up and down with sharp-eyed interest, Damian walked away, questioning his sanity. This young woman was not available to him for a liaison. His usual choice of married women or widows who asked little of him beyond satisfying their mutual desires was by far the most sensible. Never an innocent. And despite her bluster, he believed Lady Diana to be that. She'd attended the Season to find a husband, no matter what she had told Sir Charles. Dallying with her, with no intention of marrying her, was not only morally wrong, it risked him finding himself facing the parson's mousetrap. But he expected to be back in Lisbon before the month was out, well before the temptation to discover more of Lady Diana's charms threatened to overcome his good sense.

Trying to come to terms with how out of sorts he'd felt of late, he supposed that now that death so often danced at his heels, he sought something more vital and alive in his life. And Lady Diana had seemed happy for a fleeting moment during the dance. Could he make her happy like that again? He'd like to try. Or was it too soon after the loss of her friend? A ride in the park, and perhaps a stolen kiss, should the opportunity arise, wouldn't hurt, would it? He shook his head, bemused by the direction of his thoughts.

A friend, Garth Camberwell, laughed as he joined him, slapping him on the back. "I've never seen you stunned by a woman, Damian. Tread carefully, or you'll be married before you know it."

Was his interest in Lady Diana so obvious to everyone? He must get control of himself. "Not I, Garth. Let's find a waiter." He grimaced, looking for a footman, with little confidence of securing a whiskey.

"Scovell wishes to speak to you. He's in the library."

"Very well. Lead the way."

In the imposing, book-filled library, the smell of leather bindings and beeswax fought with the aromatic smoke from Scovell's cigar. Two men Damian knew from Horse Guards sat opposite him.

Scovell looked up at their entrance. "Ah, Ballantine, Camberwell. Pour yourselves a drink and join us."

Garth declined and took a chair.

Arranged on a silver tray, a variety of bottles and crystal decanters caught Damian's attention as he went to the sideboard. Returning with a whiskey, he took the comfortable, upholstered chair beside Garth's. A deep sip of the alcohol warmed its way down his throat as Scovell spoke.

"We arrested a Frenchman who has confirmed a nest of spies here in London." He stroked his moustache, his eyes grim. "Unfortunately, the information he gave us concerning their hiding place has proved useless. They keep on the move, which makes it difficult to round them up. We are looking into the most prominent British supporters of Bonaparte. The Whigs who oppose the government's determination to see the Bourbons restored to power. Baron and Baroness Holland, are known to be followers of Bonaparte, and recently entertained Frenchmen at their home in Kensington. Their naivete and admiration of Bonaparte would make them useful to the French." Exhaling cigar smoke, he nodded to Damian. "Ballantine, I believe you would be in the best position to investigate them. Find out if the Holland's affection for our enemy has turned treasonable, and if there are dangerous people we should know about among their friends." He clamped on his jaw. "Is it too much to hope that we might find the spies in their company? That they have yet to smuggle the documents over to Bonaparte? It might not be too late to retrieve them before that happens."

"What if they already suspect me?" Damian asked. "They could have been behind the attempt to hold up my coach."

"One can't be sure, but I doubt it. Not their style. More likely just a couple of wastrels hoping to fill their pockets," Scovell said. "But if the spies have become suspicious of you, that could stir the pot and force them to act."

So he was to be a lure. He must remain wary. If the stolen plans were here in London, he'd do his best to find them.

"I've arranged for an invitation for you to a house party at Holland House on Saturday," Scovell said. "The few days give you time to find out what goes on there. If there is anything relating to this theft, I'm sure you'll discover it."

"I'll do my best, sir."

"Be doubly careful and report as often as you see fit." Scovell rose and stubbed out his cigar.

Damian finished his drink, put down the glass, and rose. Garth joined him and they filed out of the library to return to the ballroom. "Sounds like it could get nasty. Watch your back, old friend."

"It's not my intention to die from a traitor's bullet on English soil if I can help it," Damian said with a chuckle. But the thought gave him pause. This was not the war he wanted to fight. Because he was his father's heir, the former earl had been strongly against Damian joining the army after he'd left university and had refused to buy him a commission. But, stultified by country life and yearning for excitement, when he'd met a fellow at Oxford who'd put this proposition to him, Damian had seen a chance to play his part in the war and grabbed it. After all, Luke could step into his shoes, should anything happen to him. This clandestine option suited him, although he believed facing the enemy on a battlefield was a nobler way to die. Some people, including Wellesley, who heavily depended on the spies' intel, nonetheless viewed them with disdain.

Regrettably, it appeared he would have to give up his gentle pursuit of the fetching Lady Diana. The depth of disappointment this caused surprised him. There were many delightful ladies in London, many ripe for an affair, should he need a distraction. Besides, had he not told himself it wouldn't be a good idea to pursue Lady Diana?

Damian went in search of her to explain why he could not meet her in the park. But she had left the ball. Too risky to send her a note. He hoped the lady would forgive him.

Chapter Three

PROMPTLY, AT NINE o'clock on Saturday morning, Diana cantered her horse down leafy Rotten Row with Briggs, her father's groom riding behind her at a discreet distance. Hyde Park lacked the challenge of galloping across the fields in the country. The dull ride was mind-numbing, but the exercise helped her keep her mind from dwelling on Anne. The cool air smelled of damp earth from a recent rain shower and gray clouds threatened more rain. There were few riders about, the usually busy South Carriage Drive almost deserted. Most of the *ton* slept late after a demanding night of engagements. A few gentlemen cantered past her as she rode, but Ballantine was not among them. Nor did he appear after she'd spent longer than she should have, waiting for him to arrive, especially when her father planned to leave within a few hours to attend the house party at Holland House. Finally, her face hot with indignation, she rode back to the stables, humiliated. Ballantine cared so little that he had not bothered to rise from his bed to meet her. She would not return to the park on Monday, hoping to see him. Fortunately, the house party was to last several days, so the temptation wouldn't arise.

In her bedchamber at their Mayfair home, she quickly changed from her habit to the green carriage gown while her lady's maid, Tims, added the last few things to her trunk.

Despite her disappointment in Ballantine failing to meet her, while she tied the strings of her bonnet, her mind remained stubbornly on him. He wore his clothes with a casual elegance. There was none of the carefully turned out Bond Street beau about him. It was the purposeful expression in his eyes and the rich timber of his voice that drew her and caused a tingling in the pit of her stomach. Despite his powerful build, he had a lithe grace, as if confident in his own skin, but she didn't find him arrogant. Diana had hoped he could be "the one," which made his casual dismissal of her hurt even more.

She must search immediately for another gentleman, before her father surprised her with someone new from his list of suitors. Why were they always so disappointing? Too old, too fat, or chinless. One gentleman smelled of mothballs and snuff. Another had a foul breath. The one who'd been presentable, one might even say handsome, had repelled her when he'd stared over her shoulder as they'd danced. As if no effort had been necessary to win her. Horrified at marrying such a man, she'd behaved in a manner sure to dissuade him from the notion. She sighed. No one she'd met thus far could compare to Ballantine. Dancing with him had been sublime. The first time she'd been distracted from thinking of Anne. A rake, she had to remind herself, hoping it would dampen her attraction to him. Obviously, one could never trust rakes, or anything they said.

Well, he didn't want her. She'd learned that lesson well and would move on to another who caught her eye. Unfortunately, it would be difficult to find one to measure up to Ballantine, whose attitude to marriage made him perfect, apart from his other excellent qualities which would prove useful in her search. But she remained undaunted. If she must share her life with someone she could never love, she intended to enjoy every moment of her freedom beforehand. And a lover would be more likely to agree to help her to find Anne. As long as he wasn't a stiff-necked fellow who was intent on being correct in all things. Like those her father seemed to find for her. Diana thought them about as attractive as limp lettuce. Any lover she chose must be at least attractive to her. Although perhaps not as much as Lord Ballantine was.

She huffed, still disappointed he had failed to keep their appointment. She simply didn't have time for suitors. Her plan must be put into action before too much time had passed, and before Papa decided she must marry his current favorite. Where Anne was concerned, she didn't have a moment to spare! Too much time had passed already, and with all of these social engagements, she hadn't had the freedom to attempt further investigation. Would the gentleman she sought be found at Holland House?

Two footmen took her trunk. Diana cast a quick glance in the cheval mirror. Satisfied with her appearance, she followed the footmen down.

Late that afternoon, she traveled with her father and grandmama in the coach. The two maids traveled with Papa's valet in other carriage. The coach wended its way through the London streets to Holland House in Kensington, in a pleasing rural setting surrounded by green meadows and acres of sloping lawns. Once through the gates, the coach proceeded along a driveway bordered by trees and flowering shrubbery. A gust of wind stirred the leaves, and for some reason, a shiver of apprehension ran down her spine. As if something unexpected and exciting awaited her here.

"I must have a fire lit in my bedchamber," Grandmama said. "Remember my rheumatism, Frederick."

"I'll order it immediately, Mama." Her father removed his hat and smoothed a hand over his thick, silvery-brown hair, which still held a few streaks of burnished gold.

Their coach joined several others in a queue, waiting to deposit guests before the rambling, Gothic-styled old brick, stucco, and stone house, where footmen rushed about opening doors and carting away luggage.

Lady Holland's house party promised a few days of pleasant company, as the Hollands invited the best poets, orators, and musicians. And there would be dancing. Papa had suggested some guests who might be of interest to her and voiced his opinion of the poet, Lord Byron. *"He is a freethinker who expresses some sound theories, although I cannot agree with some of the things he does,"* he'd said. "The ladies fawn over Byron's romantic verse," he added, as their coach jolted forward.

Grandmama patted the turban she'd first worn in 1790, which she'd insisted was still fashionable. "He behaves appallingly. The things they write about him in the newssheets are quite shocking!"

Diana believed Grandmama enjoyed salacious gossip more than she was prepared to admit. "I would like to meet him," Diana said, horribly restless and looking for a distraction. She loved the bard's poetry. As well as how controversial he was.

As they waited to alight, she peered out the window at the extensive gardens. A few sheep grazed on the lawns, painting a rustic picture. She wondered about the history of the old house and the Holland family who lived here. Considering that Henry Fox, the third Baron Holland, and Lady Elizabeth Holland were known supporters of Bonaparte, she wondered why her father had been invited. Perhaps because he was an artist of some renown. While she'd never heard him disparage the French general, she could not believe her father shared the Hollands' views. She was completely behind Wellesley in his determination to remove Bonaparte from the world stage.

The horses finally pulled up before the imposing façade and a footman hurried over to assist them. Once her feet were on the ground, she looked around with a jolt of excitement. The rambling house in the intricate Jacobean style had stood for hundreds of years. Guests roamed the decorative, arched walkways along the front façade. Several turrets were framed against the sky high above.

It was a fascinating place. Her heart raced at the thought of finding someone here who might fit her needs. He would have to be exceptional, she decided, willing, and able to help her. She attempted to push thoughts of Lord Ballantine away again and failed miserably. Surely, after such a brief acquaintance, she could relegate him to the past.

In the hall, her father caused the usual fuss, ladies curtseying low and gentlemen bowing. Diana looked about the hall with interest, where three stone archways led into the interior of the house. The staircase was of intricately carved wood, the lacy effect on the plaster walls like nothing she'd seen before. What an unusual old mansion it was. Rather mysterious and romantic, which appealed to her, having been stirred by the romantic poets. People moved around her, directed to their chambers. Papa left her and Grandmama to converse with a gentleman whose wife blushed and batted her eyelashes at Papa. Women could be so foolish around her father.

While her grandmother engaged a woman in conversation, Diana glanced up at the guests descending the staircase. A tall, dark-haired man appeared walking along the landing above. Her pulse leaped. Ballantine, here? Framed by the low balustrade, he caught the eye of several ladies present in his dark-blue tailcoat and crisp, white cravat, a gray-and-white patterned waistcoat and buff-colored pantaloons. Diana patted her hair into place, afraid her bonnet had disordered its neat arrangement, and dragged in a gusty breath. Was this the reason he hadn't come to meet her at the park? He might have sent a message. She would not allow him to see how his casual treatment of her had hurt and disappointed her.

HIS PORTMANTEAU UNPACKED, Damian approached the stairs. The decorated woodwork and arched doorways lent a slightly eastern appearance to the house interior. Bright Eastern carpets added to the impression. It was a blend of elegance and shabby indifference. Below, the hall filled with guests where servants directed them like herded sheep. Doors opened and closed on the floors above. The Hollands had invited quite a crowd. The chance of uncovering a French spy among the guests, should one even be here, would not be so easy. But he'd enjoy the Whigs' conversation, although his views were more inclined to favor the Tories. Scovell had inveigled an invitation for him, despite Damian's father having been a dyed-in-the-wool Tory. Damian's political views were not known. He kept his opinions to himself. He seldom attended the House of Lords and avoided political intrigues, preferring to carry out his work behind the scenes. But as his host had invited him to join him for a welcome drink, Damian descended the staircase in search of the salon.

He stepped onto the floor of the hall which was clearing now as guests disappeared into the interior rooms or ascended the stairs to their appointed chambers. A young lady shed her pelisse and handed it and her bonnet to a servant. She smoothed the skirts of her pale, green-and-cream-striped gown and turned to look at him. Damian groaned softly under his breath. Lady Diana, a distraction he didn't need when he must keep his head clear. But that might not be so difficult, he realized, as she frowned at him.

He crossed the intricately patterned tiles and stood before her to make his bow. "Lady Diana, how good to see you." It was no lie. Looking into her indigo-blue eyes was like diving into a deep pool. Not a gentle, nor a welcoming one, however.

She raised golden-brown eyebrows. "How surprising to find you here, Lord Ballantine." She looked past him. "If you'll excuse me, I must speak to Lady Holland."

He put up a hand to stay her but didn't try to touch her. "A moment, if you please, Lady Diana."

She hid it well, but she was angry with him. The promised meeting in Rotten Row. He hadn't forgotten but couldn't have disclosed to her why he hadn't been able to appear. Damian was always cautious of drawing the ire or interest of fathers with young, marriageable daughters. And at twenty-nine, he was often the target of matchmaking mothers. But he'd hurt Diana's feelings and disliked how that made him feel.

"I relish this opportunity to apologize to you for failing to meet you in Hyde Park. Matters beyond my control prevented it." Damian smiled but saw no corresponding smile on her firm lips. His gaze lingered there. Then rose to meet hers. "It disappointed me not to have seen you." The confession was out before he'd thought better of it.

"I had quite forgotten all about it," she said with a careless shrug. "I'm relieved to hear you didn't go to the park. As I couldn't keep our appointment myself."

The expression in her eyes dared him to question her. A corner of his lip quirked up while he fought not to chuckle. It was as much as he deserved. But where would they be now, should they have met and ridden down Rotten Row together? With every occasion he saw her, learned more about her, the harder it would be to resist her. Even now, he would like to see her alone. To kiss those soft lips, which pouted at him, and make her smile. But of course, that was impossible. He bowed again. "Ah, I see Lady Holland has come into the hall. I trust I will see you again?" Where they would be surrounded by a large group of people. Safe from temptation.

"Perhaps. I find much here to capture my interest. I'm especially keen to see the gardens. There are three fountains. One of the fountains that I'm particularly interested in viewing is decorated with marble cherubs and dolphins." Having successfully relegated him to something of less interest than a fountain, she bobbed a small curtsey and left him to join her father, who spoke to Lady Holland.

Although it unsettled him, it would be best for the lady to remain aloof from him. Easier for him to keep his distance. He had much to concern himself with during the few days here, while watching his back. Even during a genial house party, it wasn't beyond the bounds of possibility that someone would take the opportunity to knife him in the ribs while he was distracted. No one was safe in this ruthless game of spies. He felt severely hamstrung. He did not know who that might be among the diverse people here. As Scovell had said, some were Bonaparte supporters, and some of them were more actively involved than others. He must forget Lady Diana's pursed, very kissable mouth and her golden-brown lashes, which had brushed her cheek while she'd hidden her outrage from him. Whatever she led him to believe, she had been in the park and must have been deeply offended when he'd failed to turn up. With a frustrated shake of his head, he turned and walked through one of the arched doorways.

The popular heir to a viscountcy, William Lamb, walked ahead of him. Damian followed him along the corridor. The center of Whig social circles, one could always rely on Lamb for valuable information, and Damian liked him. He felt sympathetic toward him. Lamb must have been uncomfortable to find Byron here. The poet had had a very public affair with Lamb's wife, Lady Caroline, last year, who'd described him somewhat colorfully as *"Mad, bad, and dangerous to know"* in her diary. But Lamb was ambitious and made of sterner stuff. While matters might grow tense, Damian didn't expect to see a duel fought in the gardens. Although one had happened here, he'd been told. They'd erected an antique Roman altar on the site where Lord Camelford and Captain Best had fought a duel in 1804, resulting in the death of Lord Camelford.

Lamb turned and saw him. "My good fellow, are you joining Lord Holland in the salon?"

"Indeed, I am. I gather you know where to find it?"

Lamb smoothed his brown, curly hair. "It's a rabbit warren of rooms. I sent a servant to discover it." He waved a hand to encompass the wide hall where statues lurked. "He informed me it's in this direction."

"Curious old house. I'm not sure what I make of it," Damian said as they walked along a corridor.

"Or its owner," Lamb murmured enigmatically. He turned to look at Damian with a wry twinkle in his eye.

Damian focused on the possibility of a spy among them as they entered the cavernous reception room, where a group of gentlemen gathered. Samuel Rogers, the poet and art collector, occupied a seat next to Lord John Rowntree, the parliamentarian with clever, observant eyes. Richard "Conversation" Sharpe stood addressing the room. A witty, knowledgeable man, he could converse on any subject, be it metaphysics, poetry, politics, scenery, or paintings. The Thomas Grieve, Viscount Montgomery, sat with his arms folded and inclined his fair head in welcome. There were two men whom Damian didn't know.

Holland, ever the genial host, introduced Damian to the room. Damian recognized the stocky, bespectacled John Allen, who spent a good deal of his time here and was known as "Holland House Allen," a political and historical writer, and the Holland House librarian. The two strangers were French, and they rose to shake his hand. Charles Moreau had a round face and light eyes. He was almost completely bald, with tufts of gray hair sprouting above his ears. His full-lipped mouth hinted at indulgence, but his handshake was strong. The other Frenchman, Jean-Claude de La Touche, Damian knew was the son of a surgeon from Meaux with the olive skin and black hair of his countrymen. His black eyes were enigmatic, but his mouth, pressed in a hard line, revealed something of a rigid character. His hand barely touched Damian's fingers before he withdrew it. Damian knew de La Touche had been providing information to the government for some years, although much of what he'd supplied had proven of little use.

Damian took a spare seat. Was he in the presence of a French spy, or might there be two? Or might he find nothing of use here? He leaned back in his chair and crossed his legs. The conversation at least would be far from dull. Already, disagreements arose, voicing concerns about the government's latest unpopular bill.

Two hours later, Damian left the salon, having gained nothing of interest from the Frenchmen. Lady Diana returned to his mind. He shook his head, bemused. He'd become quite disciplined over the last few years. His head ruled his heart when he was engaged in dangerous work. There was no room for romance. And yet he still glanced into the drawing room as he passed to see if she was there. Knowing was one thing; apparently, turning off his desire for her was another.

Chapter Four

EAGER TO SEE more of the estate, Diana persuaded her reluctant grandmother to take a walk through the sweetly perfumed gardens.

They passed a pretty bed bordered with clipped hedges and planted with bright, spring blooms. "Lady Holland is very fond of dahlias. I can't say I share her enthusiasm." Grandmama glanced up at the sky. "I think it's going to rain."

The sun peeped from behind the wispy clouds.

"Are you growing tired, Grandmama?"

"No. Why are those in their twilight years always asked if they're tired?"

Because they often are, Diana thought. "I do not wish to fatigue you, Grandmama." She gazed at the old lady with amused affection. "Before we return to the house, shall we visit the antique Roman altar where Lord Camelford and Captain Best dueled?"

Grandmama perked up. "I knew Camelford. Pitt, as he was then. A complex man, given to violent impulses, but capable of the most noble acts of generosity." Her soft, gray-blue eyes brightened at the memory. "He was adventurous and charming with the ladies, which foolishly resulted in his death. He and Best argued over a woman." She shook her head. "He must have known that Captain Best was a crack shot."

The path took them to the impressive monument with two large pillars built above the fountain. They climbed the staircase. At the top, Diana read out the Latin inscription. *"HOC DIS MAN VOTO DISCORDIAM DEPRECAMUR."*

"Can you decipher it, Diana?" Grandmama asked.

"Papa insisted I learn a little Latin. I think it says something like *May the earth rest lightly on you.*"

"But I wonder if it did," Grandmama said enigmatically.

Diana turned to her. "Did what?"

Grandmama looked at her impatiently. "The earth resting lightly upon him."

"Why would it not?"

"Camelford's body mysteriously disappeared from a crypt in St. Anne's Church, in Soho."

"My goodness. How extraordinary."

"Yes, they never discovered where the body is or who took it."

The breeze fanned out the spray from the fountain below and dampened Diana's cheeks as they descended the stone steps.

Spying a seat nestled in a flowery bower, Diana led her grandmother to it, to rest before they made their way back to the house.

As they sat peacefully together, contemplating the beauty of the meadow before them, voices drifted down from somewhere above them.

Spoken in the French language. Diana was fluent in French, but their voices were hushed. She could only pick up a word or two when a gust of wind carried their voices this way.

Grandmama, a little hard of hearing, sat without comment as Diana, on the edge of the wooden seat, strained to grasp a sense of their words. She wished she could stand and try to see who they were, but they would see her. Three voices. One man, although fluent in French, she suspected was an Englishman because of his accent. There appeared to be two Frenchmen speaking. Tense, Diana leaned forward and heard a few more words. They sent a chill through her. "Ballantine" and then, *"traité sévèrement."* What did they mean? Ballantine was to be severely dealt with? Who were these men? Had her translation been right? If only she'd heard more. She could not have made a mistake about his title. Should she tell him? Surely, she couldn't just ignore it?

Their voices grew fainter. They must have been moving away. Then silence. Diana leaped up. "We must return to the house." She grasped her grandmother's arm to help her to her feet.

"You are so impatient," Grandmama said crossly. "Don't rush me."

Diana tucked her arm through Grandmama's and led her toward the house, although they still moved at a snail's pace. "I'm sure it's time for tea to be served. We don't want to miss it."

"Well, that is the most sensible thing you've said today." Taking Diana by surprise, Grandmama removed her arm and hastened along the path.

In the hall, a footman directed them to the drawing room, where they served afternoon tea to the ladies. Having seated her grandmother, Diana turned to leave the room.

"Where are you going, Diana? Tea hasn't been served," Grandmama called after her.

"I'll be back in a moment," Diana said, heading for the door.

Behind her, Grandmama spoke to a lady seated next to her on the sofa. "Young people today, always rushing about...so different from when we were young."

Diana slipped from the room. Her grandmother's memory must have been poor, she thought wryly, as she tried to find her way to the salon in the maze of corridors where she expected Ballantine to be. She'd heard the stories about her wily grandmama from her mother. How Grandmama had foiled her own father's plans and married the love of her life. Diana believed she took after her.

She listened at the salon door. Men were talking, but she

didn't hear Lord Ballantine's distinctive voice. Was he in there? What could she tell him? Having considered it, she wondered if she was rushing headlong into something that should not concern her. That would annoy him. She could not identify those men speaking French above where she'd sat with Grandmama. But since they hadn't spotted them when they'd climbed the steps, it seemed likely they'd been hiding somewhere. Their words, if she'd heard correctly, had shocked her. What if she was wrong? Would Ballantine consider it to be nonsense? She shrugged. It was a small price to pay, surely. She grasped the latch and turned it.

DAMIAN, BORED WITH the overblown political rhetoric spoken at length by one gentleman, considered a polite way to quit the group when the door opened.

Lady Diana popped her head in with a bright smile. "Please excuse me, gentlemen. Oh, there you are, Lord Ballantine. They have asked me to fetch you."

Damian's eyebrows shot up, but he stood quickly, wondering who the devil "they" were. He bowed. "Please excuse me, gentlemen."

The door closed behind him, and he joined her in the corridor. "Who wishes to see me?"

"I do. I have an urgent matter to discuss. Let's find somewhere to talk where we won't be overheard."

Surprised, and a little amused, he looked into her pretty face. "What is this urgent matter, Lady Diana?"

She shook her head and put a finger to her lips.

He sighed and took her arm, drawing her farther down the corridor. Reaching the library, he opened the door. As it was empty, he led her inside. Shutting them in, he turned to her. "Now, please, what this is all about?"

She quickly related what she had overheard. "I felt it was

necessary to inform you. But my interpretation could be wrong, I only…"

He gazed at her uneasily, resisting the urge to rub the prickles on his neck. "Tell me what you can." Could these be the men he sought? If so, they had him in their sights and would stop at nothing or no one who got in their way. Not even a duke's daughter should they become aware of her. Dear Lord, she must not become involved in this. He tightened his jaw. "Was any other name mentioned apart from mine?"

Her anxious eyes roamed his face. "I don't know. I heard only bits of their conversation. It was very breezy, and with Grand-mama beside me…"

"Describe them."

She clasped her hands together. "I didn't see them. They stood somewhere above us on the top of the monument. If I'd stood up to look for them, Grandmama would have unwittingly given us away." She firmed her lips and glared at him. "I hope you don't think I'm being overly dramatic. I can assure you…"

"How long ago was this?"

"Less than an hour. We came straight back here to the draw-ing room."

He felt tempted to dismiss her news as unimportant, to pro-voke her into getting upset with him, and make her lose interest. But dash it all, that wouldn't work. He suspected Lady Diana was a determined woman, and right now, she looked as keen as mustard to become involved. Of course, he couldn't let her.

"Where is your grandmother now? Did she also overhear these men?"

"No. Grandmama is a little hard of hearing. She's taking tea in the drawing room."

"Good. Join her there and leave the matter to me. Don't make so much of this. I'm sure it is nothing."

"Nothing? Surely, you don't believe that?" She shivered. "Could they mean to hurt you?"

He chuckled. "It would be foolish to jump to conclusions

after overhearing a couple of words, Lady Diana. And they were not, as you have said, mentioned in the same sentence."

"There's more should you wish to hear it." She crossed her arms across her full bosom and waited with an ironic expression.

Her feminine scent drifted across to him. Damian looked into her eyes, feeling decidedly off kilter. "There's more?"

"At least one man was undoubtedly English. Although he was certainty fluent in the French language." She tilted her head. "One would suspect he might have lived for a time in France, perhaps?"

"That is quite a leap. Many English people speak fluent French, as you obviously do yourself."

"There was a distinct difference in the rhythm of his speech. And his accent is different too."

This was interesting. Damian would advise Scovell and await his instructions. In the meantime, he would do a little digging of his own. "You are most observant, Lady Diana," he said. "Don't think that I'm not appreciative." He waved toward the door. "Allow me to escort you back to the drawing room."

She made no move to leave the library, her big eyes searching his and continuing to distract him. "Why are these people talking about you in such clandestine circumstances, Lord Ballantine?"

"Perhaps someone has taken a set against me," he said, touched by her concern and fighting the urge to take her by the shoulders and kiss her. She cared enough to come find him and tell him about it, after all. "Maybe I bettered them at card play."

She scowled at him. "Surely, this is not a laughing matter. What if you are in danger?"

"All the more reason for you to forget what you heard. You have told me. I shall deal with it, should it require any action on my part. But I would much prefer you to enjoy your stay here."

"How patronizing. Don't worry your little head about it, in other words." With a look of disgust, she turned toward the door.

He stepped closer and caught her arm to stop her. "I would never patronize a lady, especially not one as smart as you."

At his words, Lady Diana looked faintly mollified for a moment. "Does that mean that you will…?"

"No!"

Lady Diana glared at him, obviously not prepared to give him an inch. She stood close to him. Too close. He turned the latch and, aware of the scented warmth of her body, reached around her to push open the door.

She sailed out, chin high.

He followed and glanced up and down the empty corridor. "Say nothing about this to anyone, not even your grandmother," he called after her, wishing he hadn't weakened. That he'd made his argument more forceful.

"Of course I won't," she said over her shoulder.

With deep regret, he watched her bottom swaying as she crossly walked away. Could he rely on her to let the matter drop? He believed so. Lady Diana was smart. She would know better than to speak of this to anyone who could endanger them both. But he was less sure she'd leave him to deal with it alone. He should have been smarter, more convincing. Why was it so difficult to keep a clear head around her? Probably because all the blood rushed from his brain to other parts of his body.

With a muffled curse, he made his way back to the salon, where the men still continued their intense discussions. During the time he had been in the room, more had entered, while a few others had left.

Once seated, he studied those who might be of interest. And those he could cross off the list of people she could have overheard. Close to a dozen men had been in the room with him at the time. Many of the others he eliminated for other reasons. He remembered the Frenchmen, Moreau, and de La Touche had left the room before him. There were few French here. Could one of them be one of the men Lady Diana had overheard? It was certainly possible. But right now, he was more concerned with discovering the identity of the Englishman, should her observations prove true. He glanced casually around the room. Was he of interest to anyone here? Did anyone here harbor malevolent intentions concerning him? Impossible to believe it of the men around him. Might this Englishman be the one who'd gained access to the war office, where an important dispatch had recently gone missing? It would have been virtually impossible for either of these Frenchmen, with their heavy accents and Gallic appearance, to pull it off at Horse Guards.

And why target him? When had he become a threat to these men? Information must have leaked from Scovell's office about him, too.

The convivial Baron Holland rose from his chair. "Shall we join the ladies in the drawing room for a glass of wine or coffee, gentlemen?"

The parliamentarian Lord Rowntree struck up a conversation with Damian as they filed out of the room. He spoke of the diverse entertainment on offer. "The baron and baroness can be relied upon to put on a good show," he said as they walked along the corridor. He turned to Damian, his eyes sharp. "I saw you go into the library with Lady Diana Stafford. Be careful there. Her father has his sights on some gentleman he wants for her. To calm her down, the duke says." He laughed. "A bit ungovernable, apparently."

"I do not know her well," Damian said crisply. "The lady merely asked me for advice." He walked ahead to avoid further conversation.

When he entered the drawing room, Lady Diana was beside her grandmother. She gave him a studied look before glancing away. Did she think he'd made light of her discovery? It would keep her at arm's length. He should have been glad of it—but somehow wasn't.

The dark-haired poet, Lord Byron, limped into the room favoring his club foot. An appreciative murmur rose from the ladies. He smiled at them before his sensual, brown gaze settled on Lady Diana, sparking with interest.

Damian frowned. He should have welcomed it. Byron could

be the perfect distraction for the duke's daughter. The man was renowned for his affairs as much as his romantic poetry. Damian groaned inwardly. Surely, that wasn't a twinge of jealousy he felt?

Annoyed with himself, Damian clamped down on his jaw. He must deny this attraction. There was no way he would risk Lady Diana's life, even if it meant walking away from something that could be special.

Chapter Five

Her tense back pressed against the sofa cushions, Diana watched Lord Ballantine enter the drawing room with several men a few steps behind him. Had what she'd told him concerned him more than he was prepared to admit? He'd made it clear he did not want her involved. She should do as he'd suggested and not bother him again. It would allow her to continue her search for a suitable gentleman. Regrettably, the murky world she suspected Ballantine inhabited ensured that he was not a suitable subject for a liaison. But that didn't prevent her from being filled with curiosity about that world, and her lively mind wouldn't let go of the matter.

She realized, suddenly, that Lord Byron had addressed her from his seat opposite and was waiting for a reply. How rude of her! She had no clue what he'd said or even if it required an answer. A moment passed as she gazed blankly at him, hoping he would continue. His attractive, brown eyes widened. Was she the only woman he'd met who had not hung upon his every word? She suspected she was, and at any other time, she would have relished the opportunity to talk to him. "I enjoyed 'Childe Harold's Pilgrimage' immensely, my lord," she said hurriedly, by way of apology.

He nodded with a pleased smile before a lady laid a hand on his arm and distracted him, inquiring as to when they might see the third canto published, for she simply could not endure the wait. While the two discussed the poem, or rather, Byron did and the woman, in a frilly gown of pea-green lace, rapturously hung on every word, they left Diana free to study the group of men and women who seated themselves around Ballantine and engaged in cordial conversation. Women seemed to take to Ballantine as they did her father, Diana thought, a little disgruntled. But she couldn't really blame them. Papa and Lord Ballantine were both attractive, interesting men, when so many— she glanced around the room—were not.

She forced herself to concentrate. Might the two whose murmured conversation she had overheard at the monument be here in this very room? There were two Frenchmen here, which was unusual in and of itself. The moon-faced man seemed amiable enough as he chuckled and flirted with the ladies. Surely, it could not be him? The other one certainly looked more the part with his narrow, dark face, heavy eyebrows, and coal-black eyes. He spoke with a heavy French accent. She thought he looked dangerous. But were spies always what they seemed? Listening to his voice failed to jog her memory. She studied both of them, but in the end was none the wiser.

Her gaze turned to the rest of the men. Who might the French-speaking Englishman be? Surely, he would be here? But again, her contemplation of each of them gave her no clue. It was impossible to pick him out from the other erudite Englishmen present. If only she had caught a glimpse of them at the monument. It occurred to her they might return to their meeting place to continue their discussion. If she noticed one of them leaving, she would follow him and hide somewhere nearby where she could clearly hear their conversation. But how would she know when they planned for it to take place? And she could hardly drag Grandmama all the way to the fountain a second time. She would become suspicious, and it would be foolish to underestimate her powers of observation. When Grandmama wished to apply them, she was formidable.

As Diana's thoughtful gaze wandered, Ballantine caught her eye and frowned.

She raised her shoulders in a slight shrug. If he cared so much about what she thought, or what she might do, surely there must be more to this than he was prepared to tell her?

The butler came to the door. "My lords, ladies, and gentlemen, dinner is served."

As her father escorted her grandmother into the dining room, Lord Ballantine took a firm hold of Diana's arm. "Allow me, Lady Diana," he said, his smile failing to reach his eyes.

"Why glower at me?" Diana asked in an undertone as guests followed, chatting behind them. "You might let me help. I can move about unnoticed by the men."

"You think so?" Ballantine huffed out a humorless laugh. "I'd rather you didn't."

"I am aware of your sentiments on the matter," she said, annoyed that he found her amusing.

Underneath a magnificent crystal chandelier, the long dining table, covered by white linen, had been prepared for more than forty people. Silver and crystal sparkled in the candlelight.

With a nod to dismiss the footman who waited beside her chair, Lord Ballantine assisted her to be seated. He bent over her as he pushed it in. "I trust you to remain aware of it. I should not like to keep reminding you," he said in a whisper, his wine-scented breath warming her ear.

Diana gazed up at his set expression. At the hard lines bracketing his mouth. His gritty voice carried a warning, which should have deterred her. Her pulse raced. Lord Ballantine had confirmed her suspicions. Knowing she'd been right to warn him made her feel validated and a little smug. But why must he deal with this alone? She could be of assistance to him, as she'd told him. If only he realized it. But it would be foolish to try to persuade him while he flatly refused to listen. If she could find out something more, she would have something to bargain with. Until then, this mystery would give her purpose, focus, and a distraction from worrying about Anne. She watched him move around the table, chatting to the guests and taking his seat toward the bottom.

As footmen served the wine, Lord Holland rose to address the party. After dinner, they were to be treated to a recitation by Lord Byron in the blue salon.

Everyone clapped politely. Seated opposite Diana, Byron raised his glass with a smile. She had once thought Lord Ballantine a rake, but he showed little inclination to behave in that fashion, at least with her. There was a stark difference between him and the poet. Byron's very public affair with Lady Caroline Lamb had shocked many when she'd behaved so disgracefully. But he must have broken her heart. And Diana doubted he cared very much. Women were a conquest and, once he had them, he then moved on to the next. When he glanced her way, his eyes looked devilish. She didn't wish to flirt with him, nor did she wish to offend him if she failed to appear at his recital. But should either of the Frenchmen be absent, then she would go in search of them.

The footmen brought in the covers, tasty aromas filling the air. Th delicately flavored fish soup was served. A contented hum rose around the table, along with the clink of crystal glasses and silverware. Diana almost dropped her spoon when she heard an elegant, fair-haired Englishman seated across the table speak French to the moon-faced Frenchman at his right. she caught enough to believe it was nothing of interest, as indeed it wouldn't be, here. But what was Ballantine's reaction? She couldn't tell from where he sat farther down the table, and a gentleman leaning over his plate to spoon up his soup blocked her view.

She discreetly watched the Englishman, who was addressed as Viscount Montgomery by the lady on his left. He looked in his thirties and was good-looking, with fine features. The cut of his dark-blue coat spoke of Bond Street tailors, and the gilt buttons on his cream silk waistcoat and at his cuffs gave an impression of wealth. His shoulders were rather narrow, and he wasn't as broad in the chest as Ballantine. But she must concentrate on this Englishman, and not Ballantine. It was vital to find out who he was. How could she manage it discreetly? If she asked her father, he might believe her to be interested in him. She was about to discount this method when it occurred to her that if the gentleman wasn't married, he might make a perfect distraction. A suitor she had no intention of marrying who could halt Papa's search for a husband for her. That would enable her to spend time with him and learn all about him. But she could not be sure it was he she sought until she'd heard him speak French again without the surrounding noise.

WHILE HIS MIND struggled with the problem of Lady Diana, Damian conversed with Lord Franklin, the elderly gentleman with bushy, white sideburns beside him who smelled strongly of pomade and cigar smoke. It was obvious Damian's warning had not made the slightest difference. It was impossible to be brutally frank with her, not when she looked so lovely tonight. The blue satin reflected in her dark-blue eyes. He'd been too aware of the upward thrust of her bosom in the low-necked gown. He caught the scent of roses when he'd leaned over her. Instead of issuing the sharp warning he'd intended, he wanted to kiss the fragrant hollow beneath her ear, exposed by the smooth arrangement of her heavy hair, and then down her creamy-skinned neck to other glorious pleasures. With a silent groan at the eager response of his body, he admitted he was in trouble. How best to handle the persistent Lady Diana? He would have to outwit her. Not a simple task.

"Ballantine?" Lord Franklin's eyebrows rose at Damian's prolonged silence.

"It might require considerable thought," Damian said quickly, realizing he'd taken too long to answer the fellow.

Franklin nodded, thankfully satisfied with his answer.

A footman filled Damian's wine glass as the following course appeared, the steaming, flavorsome aromas of meat and vegetables blending with the smells of smoke and hot wax, as well as the ladies' perfume. Damian took a hearty sip of red wine, wishing they had not placed him at such a distance from Lady Diana. What might she throw at him next? Must he deal with these spies for Scovell, get his hands on the missing documents, while watching his back, and keeping Lady Diana safe? He swallowed the wine too fast and coughed. At least, the enormity of his task dampened his desire to discover more of Lady Diana's charms. But he feared that would not last.

"All right, Ballantine?" Franklin asked with concern.

"Quite, thank you." He held up the ruby liquid swirling in the crystal wineglass. "A fine vintage, is it not?"

AFTER DINNER, THE guests filed back into the drawing room to hear Byron read his latest work. Seated, Damian made a quick study of those present. Moreau and de La Touche were not, although it might have been because poetry failed to interest them. Lady Diana entered with her grandmother. Pleased to see her here, he spoke to the man seated on a chair beside him. But when he heard the door open and close again, he looked to where she'd been sitting. Her grandmother sat alone. *Curse it!* He excused himself and left the room.

She might have gone for any number of reasons, including something as innocuous as to fetch a shawl for her grandmother. But he couldn't take the risk. There was no sign of her in any of the reception rooms, nor, even more worrying, were there either of the Frenchmen.

As he stood in the hall, a maid appeared. She dropped into a curtsey.

"Which chamber is Lady Diana's?" he asked before she could lower her head and scurry away. "I have a message for her."

She pointed. "Three doors from the top of the stairs, milord."

"Thank you." He ran up the stairs and knocked on the door. No answer.

Damian leaned over the balustrade below; the hall was empty. He descended the stairs, grinding his back teeth. Where the devil had she gotten to? Must he play nursemaid to Lady Diana for the duration of their time here?

As he reached the hall, a footman opened the front door and admitted the lady in question. Her eyebrows rose when she saw Damian frowning at her.

She recovered herself quickly and advanced on him with a smile. "Were you planning a walk too, my lord? It's a lovely night. The smoky rooms bothered me, so I strolled along the arched walkway. The air is so sweet with spring flowers."

They walked together down the hall. She was a picture of innocence. Damian didn't believe her for a minute. "Not searching for the missing Frenchmen?" he suggested, in as pleasant a voice as hers.

She widened those blue eyes a man could drown in. "Are they missing?"

He took her arm. "Allow me to escort you to the drawing room. Lord Byron is about to begin."

She pulled back and stared at him. "You are the most stubborn man. At dinner, I heard an Englishman speaking to one of the Frenchmen in his language, the partly bald Frenchman."

"Is that so unusual?" he asked casually. But his interest piqued.

"It might be the Englishman I overheard." Her hands were akimbo, drawing her gown tight around her body and revealing the enticing curve of her hips and narrow waist. He was aware of her delicate bones, and how vulnerable she would be to ruthless men.

"Who was he?" He growled.

She blinked, surprised at his gruff demand. "I'd tell you if I knew. He has fair hair and looks to be is in his mid-thirties."

Damian nodded. "Thank you for the information." He offered her his arm. "Shall we go in?"

Making no attempt to join him, she shook her head. "I couldn't find them. But I'm sure they're out there meeting somewhere. Wouldn't you like to search for them? You might discover something of interest."

"What makes you think I'm interested?"

She made a dismissive sound with her lips. "I can see it in your eyes, Lord Ballantine."

He leaned forward and stroked a finger beneath her bottom lip. "What you see is my frustration with your stubborn intention of placing yourself in danger while fighting the desire to kiss you. And I shall give in to the impulse should we remain here a moment longer."

"Oh! You are outrageous!" With a shrug of her shoulder, she flounced ahead of him.

Damian restrained a bark of laughter and followed her. He would escort her to the drawing room, see her settled safely beside her grandmother, then undertake an exploration of the gardens.

Chapter Six

SEATED BESIDE HER grandmother, Diana nibbled her bottom lip as she watched Lord Ballantine leave the room. What had just occurred perplexed her. Ballantine's intense alertness when she'd described how Lord Montgomery had spoken French at dinner belied his insistence that she saw danger where there was none. While his threat to kiss her alarmed her, it had intrigued her far more. She'd fought to remain unaffected, but it was all she could do to turn away from him with an indifferent shrug of her shoulder. *Indifferent!* The heat in his eyes had thrilled her. Had he really meant to kiss her? He'd left her wondering what kissing him would be like. She suspected it would differ from the kisses of other men, which had always left her feeling a trifle flat. She grimaced and grew annoyed with herself. Ballantine had used the threat of a kiss to distract her. And he had succeeded admirably. Now, reacting to the information she had given him, he had left to pursue the men in the gardens without her!

"Why are you fidgeting, Diana?" Grandmama turned to observe her with a worried frown. "You are quite flushed. Are you well?"

"It is a little too warm in here, and my corset pinches," Diana whispered. It had since Ballantine had robbed her of breath.

"Then sit up straight. And don't frown. Lord Byron is about to begin. I'm surprised I have to remind you of that."

"I'm sorry, Grandmama."

Diana gazed around the room. Neither the Frenchmen nor the fair-haired Englishman had returned. *Drat!*

The flamboyant poet took his place beside the fireplace and after the scrape of chairs and the odd cough, a polite hush came over the room. How long before she could escape again? Grandmama would retire after the poetry reading and give her time to search for the men in the garden. It might be possible to catch them before they concluded their meeting. If that was what they were doing.

Her sharp intake of breath drew in the stuffy air mixed with perfume, snuff, and body odor. What if she ran into Lord Ballantine? He would be angry. He might even carry out his threat and kiss her.

"You shivered, Diana," Grandmama declared. "Don't tell me you are well. I won't believe it. Off to bed immediately, my girl, with a warming pan."

Gathering up her reticule and gloves, her grandmother rose in stately fashion before Byron could open his mouth. "My lord," she said, addressing the stunned poet, "I apologize. My granddaughter seems to have caught a chill and must retire. I hope you intend to gift us with another reading before we leave."

Byron met Diana's gaze. He looked intrigued, and he murmured something polite in reply.

Diana silently followed her grandmother from the room. She groaned under her breath when her father rose to follow them.

Grandmama approached a footman in the hall and issued her orders for a hot drink and a warming pan to be brought to Diana's bedchamber.

When they reached the staircase, her father held Diana by her shoulders, his dark-blue gaze studying her. "You feel ill, Diana?"

She felt a terrible fraud. "No, Papa. A little tired, perhaps."

"Go to bed," he said with a relieved smile. "A strapping girl like you, you'll be as fit as a fiddle tomorrow."

"I'm sure I will, Papa."

He bent to kiss Grandmama's cheek. "Good night, Mama."

"Good night, Frederick." Her grandmother gathered up her lilac skirts and mounted the stairs, with Diana following.

Grandmama entered Diana's bedchamber and fussed around her, while Tims assisted her to undress. "Is your accommodation comfortable, Tims?" Diana asked her maid as she finished brushing her lady's hair.

"Yes, my lady. I like to meet new people. The footman, James, is full of mischief and made us all laugh at supper."

"My, how noisy it must be down there in the servants' hall," Grandmama said, causing the maid to wince. "You may go, Tims."

At the knock on the door, Tims exited and the household servants brought in a cup of tea and the bed warmer. In her nightgown, Diana sipped the honey-sweetened tea and pondered why her father had seemed suddenly so concerned about her. His interest in her seldom extended to her health. Had he a suitor for her in mind here at Holland House? Her ribcage contracted at the horrible thought and made her cough.

Grandmama turned at the door. "Into bed, Diana, before you become chilled."

She watched as Diana obeyed, then left her.

Diana leaned back on the pillows and sighed. Was it safe to leave the house and try to find the men? If there was a chance to bring the murderous rogues to account, she would take the risk. She gripped the sheet. And the devil who had abducted Anne must also be found and thrown into Newgate Prison. However, it would be wise to give her grandmother a little time to settle into bed, just to be sure. The bed was delightfully warm, and her eyelids felt heavy. But at the thought of Lord Ballantine in danger, her sleepiness fled, and she threw back the covers.

Twenty minutes later, having dressed again, she crept down the stairs. It was too early for the poetry reading to have concluded. She was confident she wouldn't run into her father as she hurried to the door. Outside, the wind had freshened, blowing the branches of the trees about. The thin muslin she wore offered little protection from the cold. She shivered, pulled her shawl more tightly around her shoulders, and darted out into the night.

Head down, she hurried over the path that led between the trees, their branches swaying, a sliver of moon casting deep shadows. She slowed as she approached the tinkling fountain, the monument looming above, alert to any sound. Was that voices she heard carried on the wind?

Walking into a deep well of darkness, she banged up against a solid male body smelling of cigars and brandy.

Hands steadied her. A tall man, he drew her into where light fell from a brazier. "Lady Diana? Where are you off to in this weather?"

She looked up into the man's face, half in shadow. His hair looked silvery, but he was unmistakably the Englishman. The one who spoke perfect French. Diana swallowed, suddenly fearful. "Sir, I don't believe we have been introduced," she said stiffly, feeling a warning shiver race up her spine.

He chuckled. "Viscount Montgomery, Lady Diana. I know your father, the duke, very well. May I be of service?"

"Oh, yes, thank you, my lord. I am annoyed with myself. I lost a pearl bracelet in the gardens somewhere near the pond today and went to look for it." She pulled her shawl close. "But it's too dark, and it's a good deal cooler than I expected."

"Allow me to help you look for it."

"No, thank you. It's a foolish idea. Grandmama would be so cross if she knew I was out here," Diana said, relieved that her voice had steadied. She turned to walk back to where the towers and roofline of the enormous house stood outlined against the night sky, the lower stories throwing welcome warm lights into the gardens. She fought the urge to run.

"A sensible decision." He offered her his arm. "Allow me to escort you."

She took it reluctantly. As they neared the house, a large

shape emerged out of the dark. Lord Ballantine. His stern face was revealed in the candlelight from the hall chandelier.

"Ah, Ballantine, out for a stroll?" asked Lord Montgomery. "I have discovered Lady Diana in search of a lost bracelet. But we have given up and return to the house."

"I enjoy a walk in the night myself," Ballantine said, failing to hide that irritated tone she recognized. "But it proves a little cool for my taste."

She cast Ballantine a warning glance as a footman opened the door for her.

⊱✦⊰

As Damian and Montgomery stood in the hall watching the slim form of Lady Diana climb the stairs to her bedchamber, Montgomery turned to address him. "Not an admirer of Byron's poetry, Ballantine?"

"I am. But I found a pretty maid more alluring," Damian said.

Montgomery's icy-gray eyes widened, but his expression remained skeptical. "I must say I admire your fortitude. On such an unpleasant evening."

"I found a comfortably furnished summerhouse beside the ornamental pond," Damian said, having discovered it when carrying out surveillance of the property.

Montgomery chuckled. "An assignation so soon? You have done well. I shall keep the summerhouse in mind, should I be as fortunate."

"One might ask what brought you out tonight." Damian eyed the man he believed was not only a danger to him, but his country. He wanted to take him by the cravat and choke the truth out of him, but he had to bide his time.

"Merely the desire to blow away the cobwebs. Lord Holland's gatherings can be unrelenting." Montgomery bowed his head. "Good evening."

After Montgomery had gone up to his chamber, Damian remained in the hall, watching for any gentlemen who might emerge from the dark. He removed a cheroot from his pocket but didn't light it. Instead, he gazed up the stairs toward Lady Diana's bedchamber. His warning had been ignored, which made him feel extremely frustrated.

"Lord Ballantine!"

Hearing his name whispered, he searched the floor above. Dash it all if the duke's daughter didn't appear from behind a column.

He shoved the cheroot into his pocket and ran up the stairs. "What the devil are you up to, minx?"

"You make me sound like a child," she said with a frown. "I'm hardly that at one and twenty."

"I am well aware of your age," he said acerbically. A child would have been far less trouble.

She glanced around, then beckoned him over to the open door of her bedchamber. "Come inside," she murmured. "It's important that I speak to you."

"I am not in the right frame of mind to enter your chamber, Lady Diana."

"It's more dangerous to argue the point out here, surely."

"That wasn't the sort of danger I referred to," he said, giving up and following her inside.

He leaned against the door, keeping some distance between them. "Well? Do you intend to explain your reasons for wandering about the gardens alone at night?"

"I don't have to explain myself to you, Lord Ballantine. I thought you might like to know what I've discovered. But if not, don't let me keep you." In her nightclothes, she folded her arms across her bosom, drawing his attention to her unfettered breasts beneath the shawl.

He stepped forward, so close, she had to raise her head to look up at him. "All right. We'd best get this over with quickly. You are a fetching woman and behind you is a rumpled bed I find most inviting."

She flushed but held her ground.

He cocked an eyebrow. "Please continue. I am all ears."

"Lord Montgomery must have come from the meeting near the monument. The others were still there. I heard their voices, but again, not what was said."

"That's all you have to tell me?"

She huffed. "Don't you see? Lord Montgomery is part of it. And there are at least two other men involved!"

While he wasn't prepared to admit it, which would only encourage her, he had already discovered that for himself. Having gotten closer to their meeting place, he'd heard the three men, but they'd stood in the shadows. He'd slipped away as the meeting had broken up and the Englishman had left. It was aggravating not to hear more, but he had witnessed the rustled exchange of at least one document. Unsure who the third man was, or who now had the document in their keeping, he would have to be patient, which was not his forte, and resourceful to discover where in the house the man had stowed it. Once he left Holland House, it would be too late.

Standing before Lady Diana, he gazed down into her widened, blue eyes. She thirsted for information. It was in the way she held herself, and how her tongue darted out to touch the beguiling indent in her full top lip.

Dammit!

Damian cupped her face in his hands and, as his deep breath inhaled the warm smell of a fragrant woman, he lowered his mouth to hers, finding her luscious lips soft.

After an initial squeak of protest, Lady Diana's arms coiled around his neck. Silencing the warning of his rational mind, he deepened the kiss, delving in to touch her tongue, eager to learn the taste of her mouth. She murmured against his lips, and her fingers threaded through the hair at his nape.

Damian slid his hands down over the curve of her waist to her hips and pulled her soft, sweetly scented body closer. As his hardening erection pressed against her lower body, her eyes flew open. But she did not draw away. What was this? Did she invite him into her bed? While he deliberated the madness of such an act against his growing passion, he heard men's laughter on the stairs.

Abruptly aware of the demands of his body, Damian snapped himself back under control. He stepped away to a safe distance. "That could be your father coming to see how you are."

She flew to the wardrobe and flung open the door. "In here, quickly."

He was too large and too old to hide in cupboards. Keeping the door slightly ajar, he watched Diana climb into bed. She pulled the covers up to her neck and snuffed out the candle.

In the dark, breathing in dust and her familiar, stirring scent, he waited. The men's voices passed by this chamber and continued on, and then there was silence. With relief, he pushed open the wardrobe door in need of less stifling air and a hearty desire to escape calamity. There was a scratch at the tinder box, then a candle flame burst into life. His ardor momentarily dampened, he gazed warily at Lady Diana, who looked far too inviting beneath the covers.

He eyed her vulnerable mouth, flushed pink from his kiss. "I shall remove myself from temptation, my lady," he said as he strode to the door. "I enjoyed the kiss." A good deal more than he should have.

She clutched the bedclothes, her eyes accusing him. "But I have been of use to you, Ballantine. You must admit it."

He had missed the opportunity to see who'd come into the house. Lady Diana had prevented that. "No, you were not. You forced me to reveal my presence to Montgomery. I didn't trust him with you."

Her expression softened for a moment, then she threw back the covers and purposefully climbed from the bed. Her nightgown rode up, revealing her delicate knee, and a delightful glimpse of pearl-colored slim thigh.

Damian rubbed his hand over his eyes. *Dear Lord, give me strength!* Fighting the urge to take her to bed and settle himself between those delightful thighs, he averted his gaze, a hand firmly on the door latch. "Good evening, Lady Diana."

"Wait. I have a plan," she began earnestly, coming toward him.

"I'd rather not hear it." He opened the door and, checking no one was about, hurried out, shutting it quietly behind him.

Striding to his allotted chamber, he removed the cheroot from his pocket and clamped it between his teeth. Never mind the spies. Would he survive Lady Diana?

Chapter Seven

DIANA READIED HERSELF for bed, washing her hands and face to calm herself. She took off her slippers, taking her time, her heart still beating too fast. How Ballantine had looked at her. As if he'd wanted to see her naked. She rubbed the goose flesh on her bare arms. She had never seen such raw desire in a man's eyes before. Had he intended her to feel him hard against her when he'd pulled her close? She had warmed all over and her nipples had peaked. And she'd sighed when he'd drawn away, his musky scent lingering.

With a delicious shiver, she climbed into bed. Snuggling down, she ran her tongue over her top lip and indulged in what might have happened had he stayed. But it was beyond her limited experience to imagine it. She hadn't found it difficult to understand the gentlemen with whom she'd danced. Some had made no secret of their desire for her, while the older gentlemen had often been more avuncular. But it was difficult to penetrate the wall Ballantine had built around himself. Something tragic must have occurred in his past for him to involve himself with dangerous people. And it seemed clear to her that he did, in some capacity. The idea stirred her tender heart, even though she didn't know if it was true. Most gentlemen spent their time overseeing their estates, hunting game, attending Parliament, dancing at balls, and dining at their clubs. They married to fill their nurseries in the hopes of an heir and a spare. She doubted many undertook such work.

What a ninny she was to think she could manage even a brief liaison with Ballantine. It would consume her. And when he was done with her, because he had said emphatically he had no intention of marrying for years, he would leave her bereft and unable to appreciate any other man. It was a warning, and she should heed it.

Diana poked her pillow into a better shape and rested her head on it, staring at the circle of candlelight on the ornate ceiling. Despite her fears, she remembered how she'd felt with his arms around her. His powerful musculature, the lingering smells of smoke, brandy, and a fresh, citrusy cologne. How her head had fit just below his chin. And how he had made her feel. *Safe?* Had she ever really felt safe? Certainly not in the weeks following Anne's disappearance. Absurd when her father employed so many servants.

Whatever the reason, Diana wanted to know more about Ballantine. To be closer. To have him look at her that way again. For him to kiss her. Was she being bold or just foolish? Well, he had resisted temptation, even after they'd kissed. There might not be another chance. The thought made her feel strangely empty.

She snuffed out the candle and lay back in the dark. At least he might have listened to her plan. Ballantine was such a frustrating man. He would be aware he was in danger. Why refuse her offer of help when she was willing to perform even some insignificant but important task to aid him? Diana wished she hadn't hindered him though. He might have learned something from Lord Montgomery.

She admitted that while her initial intention had been to talk him into helping her to find Anne, now it was her fear of him dying that drove her to keep pressing him. She couldn't stand back and not save Ballantine if there were something she might do to prevent it. If anything happened to him, she wouldn't be able to bear it. Diana gasped. Was she falling in love with him?

That way led to heartbreak. It was unlikely that the man her father chose for her would break her heart. Or distract her from her own pursuits. But judging by her father's choices in suitors, what a dreary existence it would be. She sighed. Such a passionless life, and all the more reason to find a lover before she married.

She devised a plan she considered to be ingenious, convinced she should carry it out, undaunted by any objections Ballantine might throw at her. Tomorrow, while Papa was in a mood to listen to her, she would ask him about Lord Montgomery. Was he married? If he was single, her father might see the merit in such a marriage, and if so, encourage them to spend time together. If Lord Montgomery was willing, she would often be in his company. She might learn something important. And if she could distract him, it would free Ballantine to search for information vital to his cause. Whatever that cause was. If only she knew more about it. But Ballantine was a spy, she was certain. Could Lord Montgomery be a spy too? What if he worked for the French? It made her tremble to think it. She'd heard of such things.

Diana slept fitfully and in the morning had to resort to a little rouge to brighten her pale cheeks. Tims worked her skill with Diana's thick hair. Dressed in her lilac morning gown, Diana went to knock on Grandmama's door.

They went down to breakfast, passing a middle-aged gentleman in the hall. He greeted them with a stiff bow.

"That was the Earl of Cumbria," Grandmama whispered.

Diana turned swiftly to view his thin, angular frame disappear around a corner. She was horrified at how grumpy and old he appeared. Surely, her father wouldn't consider him?

They entered the smaller breakfast room, which smelled of hot food. A dozen seated guests expressed their interest in this morning's talk. A famous archeologist was to speak about the ancient marble sculptures brought recently from Greece by Lord Elgin, now in a private collection.

As they drank their tea and ate buttered toast, her father came to join them. Papa seemed in a good mood today, smiling and addressing the other guests. He ordered coffee, ham, and eggs from the footman.

As coffee was placed before him, he glanced at her. "Are you feeling better, Diana?"

"Yes, I'm well, Papa."

"After breakfast, there is someone I wish you to meet."

Diana's throat tightened, and she took a hasty sip of tea. "Oh? Who is it?" She gazed around, hoping Ballantine had come in. He hadn't.

"Lowther, Earl of Cumbria. I've arranged for us to meet him in the salon at ten."

Diana cringed inwardly. She leaned forward to appeal to him in a soft voice. "Papa, I believe you know Viscount Montgomery. I met him on the garden path yesterday, and he introduced himself to me."

Her father's breakfast arrived. He sliced into the ham and forked up some egg, gazing at her, his blue eyes alert. "Montgomery? Yes, I know him. Not well, however. Why do you ask, Diana?"

After a quick glance at her grandmother, who stared at her with suspicion, Diana hurried on. "I wondered if he was married."

"Mm," said Papa. "He's a widower. Merely a viscount. I wish for better for you. Now Cumbria…"

"Lord Montgomery is very handsome, and a good deal younger," Diana said. "Did you find him presentable?"

Grandmama sniffed. "Handsome is as handsome does."

"I thought he had elegant manners," she said, ignoring Grandmama, who made her presence felt with just a few words.

Papa seemed pleased that she showed some interest in choosing a husband. This deception was necessary, she assured herself guiltily.

"I'll introduce you formally to him tonight after dinner in the ballroom. And we shall see, eh?"

"Thank you, Papa."

"His family is respectable," he mused. "I believe his estate in Lincolnshire is prosperous. If no problem presents itself, then perhaps…"

Grandmama's teacup rattled in its saucer, and she gathered up her reticule and gloves. "I should like Diana to take her time, Frederick. She has only just met the man."

Flustered, Papa hunched his shoulders. His mother was the only one who had that effect on him. "I understand, Mama. But you know how these things are done."

"I know only too well. But I will be angry should you rush Diana into an engagement before she is entirely happy with the arrangement." She stood. "Come, Diana. It's a delightful morning and there is time for a stroll before we attend the archeologist's talk."

Struggling to find a reason she'd gone out in the gardens without mentioning it, Diana followed her grandmother from the breakfast room.

"Have we met Lord Montgomery?" Grandmama asked in the hall, turning her shrewd, blue-gray gaze upon her. "I don't recall him."

"It happened when I slipped out for a few moments," Diana confessed. "I needed some fresh air."

"Have you not a window in your chamber?"

"I do, but…"

"You like this Montgomery so much that you mentioned him to your father?"

"I have a good reason, Grandmama," Diana said miserably. She hated keeping secrets.

Grandmama's eyebrows rose. "I don't know what you're up to, Diana. I expect it is something I'd rather not know about." Her eyes softened. "You are not in the usual way, but a sensible girl for all that. I understand you wish to find someone to care for you and protect you. Someone you could love. You are no longer a young debutante who requires strict chaperoning. But please think carefully before you do anything rash." She paused, and a faraway expression stole into her eyes before she focused again on Diana. "Sometimes, when you are young, passion rules your head, and you make mistakes."

"I will be careful, Grandmama," Diana said, chastened. She wondered about her grandmother's past. Great-Grandfather had intended her to marry another gentleman before she'd met Grandfather. They'd married despite her father believing him unsuitable. Diana pondered how she could persuade Grandmama to reveal more as they walked in the gardens and strolled along the path. The sun warmed her shoulders, the air scented with perfume from a bank of white roses where contented bees hummed.

Why hadn't Ballantine come to breakfast? She had planned to dally there as long as she could, but Grandmama had whisked her off. When would she see him again? She hoped they might have time alone to talk. Although the mysterious man strongly resisted telling her what he was up to. She nibbled her bottom lip with her teeth. Time was growing short. They had only tomorrow before they returned home, and then it would be unlikely she'd see much of him, and only on formal occasions. The thought disturbed her and spurred her on to considering how she might waylay him.

"Now tell me about Lord Montgomery," Grandmama said, unexpectedly disturbing Diana's thoughts.

Caught on the hop, Diana struggled to come up with an explanation which would satisfy her grandmother. She decided on the truth. "He joined me when I was returning to the house after my walk. I found him quite charming."

"I've always distrusted overly charming gentlemen," her grandmother replied as they strolled on.

AFTER DAMIAN HAD left Lady Diana the previous evening, he'd slipped outside again in search of the other men. They might have entered the house while he'd been in her bedchamber, but there was always the chance they hadn't.

The clouds had wandered away and in the moonlight, it had been impossible to hide from prying eyes. Not until he'd reached the cover of the first copse of trees. Smoking his cheroot, he'd stridden toward the monument, sending aromatic smoke into the air while allowing himself to be seen. A Mr. Graves and his wife had come toward him along the path, laughing together. They'd greeted him, then continued on to the house.

The wind had freshened, blowing Damian's hair about. He'd shoved a lock back before it could blind him, and having reached the trees, stamped out the cheroot, veered off the path, and listened. It had been too quiet. He'd come too late. Tomorrow, in daylight, he'd search for some sign to alert him to where they'd met. A discarded cigar or cheroot or the imprint of the men's shoes on the ground would be a welcome clue. Then, if they met again, he'd be ready.

As he'd bent beneath the low bow of an elm, a sudden explosion had rent the air. The birds had flown from their roosts, squawking and erupting into the night sky. Damian had felt the heat of the ball passing within a whisker of his head. He'd crouched behind a bush, drawn out his pistol from where he'd tucked it into the back of his trousers beneath his coat, and listened. The slap of running feet had passed close to him. Unsure of the direction of the runner, Damian had waited, his pistol cocked. When nothing further had occurred, he'd stood and cautiously moved out of the bushes. He'd stepped onto the path in time to see a man enter the house. With his face obscured in the poor light, it was impossible to see much of him, not his build, nor the color of his hair. He'd quickly vanished inside. Having learned nothing useful, Damian had cursed. His stomach had tightened. Someone had almost killed him for his efforts.

Walking back to the house, he'd swung around at footsteps

behind him, his hand on the gun concealed in the back of his pantaloons beneath his tailcoat.

Charles Moreau had emerged out of the gloom and hurried over to him. "Was that a shot I heard?"

"I believe it was."

"*Mon Dieu.* That is strange. Is it wise to be outside after dark?" He'd clutched his coat closer. "Who knows what rogues might have lurked here in the gardens on the lookout for good pickings?"

Damian had joined him, matching his pace, and they'd covered the last few yards to the house. "One wonders," he'd said, his voice heavy with irony. "Someone shooting foxes, I imagine."

Moreau had failed to react to his tone. "I find the rooms in the house have grown smoky and stale. It's a shame, but I shan't go on my usual evening stroll before bed again."

Damian had opened the door and stood aside for the Frenchman to pass through. "A sensible decision."

It had been an excellent shot, he'd considered as he had climbed the stairs to his bedchamber. If he hadn't ducked under that branch, he'd have been lying dead beneath it. He would take his chance again in daylight. While Lady Diana had been correct in her interpretation of what she'd heard, he wasn't about to tell her so. She hardly needed encouragement. He'd shaken his head. If only he were free to pursue the lady. But he was forced to forget about it for several reasons, one of which was the need to stay above ground.

By the time he'd come downstairs that morning, only two women still remained in the breakfast room. Damian stirred a lump of sugar into his tea to give him energy. He could sleep anywhere, even a haystack if it came to that, but last night in his chamber, he'd lain wide awake. He'd dwelt on the identity of the shooter, looking for something important he might have overlooked. But nothing had come to mind.

Instead, Lady Diana's soft mouth beneath his, her breasts pressing against his chest, had filled his mind. Her eager response to his kiss and the sight of rumpled bedsheets smelling of warm woman almost tipped him over the edge. Would he see her during the day? *Dash it all!* It was far too perilous for them both. Lady Diana was not about to become mixed up in this. He could imagine her father's wrath, and he wouldn't blame him. He turned his mind to the more vital question of what to do next.

If he alerted Scovell to the attempt to kill him, his spymaster might pull him from the mission. Damian had no intention of leaving, not without achieving what his spymaster had sent him here to do. In addition to outing the Englishman who had infiltrated the war office, it was imperative for them to find the documents before they left these shores. He was running out of time. Wellesley and the lives of his men on the Continent depended on him succeeding. And whether he left here alive depended on discovering who that shooter was before he made another attempt.

Leaving the breakfast room, he passed the drawing room, where guests gathered to listen to the archeologist. Damian opened the door and looked in. Lady Diana was there with her grandmother. She nodded, her eyes anxious when she saw him. He was careful not to do anything to encourage her, his gaze roaming the rest of the room until he spied the Frenchman Moreau, who had appeared last night right after the gunshot. Was the man he'd seen entering the house earlier the one who'd tried to kill him? Or could it have been Moreau? The Frenchman's tightly fitted topcoat couldn't have concealed a gun, but he might have stowed it somewhere, although he didn't smell of gunpowder. Inclined to dismiss him, Damian closed the drawing room door and headed for the stairs. He would pay a visit to the Frenchman's chamber while this opportunity presented itself.

Chapter Eight

MUST WOMEN BE so sheltered from life? As if they lacked the ability to think for themselves, and the courage to deal with problems? Some women liked that, but Diana found it frustrating.

She watched the gray-haired, whiskered Professor Summer put on his spectacles and take his place at the podium. He shuffled his papers, and having organized his books and drawings, cleared his throat. "Ladies and gentlemen."

The decorative sculptures taken from the Parthenon, the ancient Doric temple on the Acropolis in Athens, proved a fascinating subject. Despite the other thoughts crowding her head, Diana found herself enthralled. When the professor's lecture, and the half hour of questions from the guests that followed, concluded, she and Grandmama went to the library, where her father waited with the gentleman he wished to introduce to her.

To her surprise, when they entered the book-filled room, which smelled of old tomes and cigar smoke, it was not Lord Lowther, the thin gentleman with a stern mouth who had made her miserable when she'd seen him earlier, but the handsome Lord Montgomery, who sat seemingly at ease beside her father on the sofa. Lord Montgomery rose as they came in and assisted her grandmother into an armchair. *Papa had listened to her!* Her relief and gratitude was followed swiftly by guilt she hastily tamped down. Diana hurried forward with a smile.

After the introductions and a polite conversation about their time spent at Holland House, her father rose to excuse himself, leaving Grandmama as chaperone.

Lord Montgomery's fair, good looks were undeniably pleasing, but Diana found his pale, blue-gray eyes oddly opaque, as if, like a submerged iceberg, he hid much of himself from her. And as she suspected him of being a murderous spy, this did not surprise her. While he attempted to charm her grandmother, Diana formed the questions she planned to ask him should she get a chance during the evening. Not gaining the warm reception from her grandmother that he might usually expect from older ladies, Lord Montgomery turned back to Diana. "Do you like to dabble in oils, Lady Diana?"

"No, my lord, I prefer to be outdoors."

"My dear wife, Mary, who sadly passed away five years ago, was a keen gardener. She loved her roses."

Diana wondered if he would be surprised to learn about her hobby of shooting pumpkins with a dueling pistol. She might have offered the information to deter him at another time, sure it would be most effective, but regrettably, that would not fit with her plan. "I love to dig the soil. But mostly, I putter around about the conservatory, repotting begonias and orchids."

He smiled approvingly.

Grandmama's eyebrows rose, but she refrained from pointing out that Diana only went to the conservatory in order to leave the house and walk to the stables.

It wasn't entirely a lie. She had once knocked a pot onto the marble floor and had been obliged to repot it. Their conversation became so polite that it was almost stilted when Grandmama offered nothing. Lord Montgomery cleared his throat and rose. Fearing she had not shown enough enthusiasm, Diana stood and offered him her hand. "I do hope we can talk again, Lord Montgomery," she gushed, batting her eyelashes. "There is dancing tonight in the ballroom. Shall we see you there?"

She offered him her hand. He kissed it, lingering for a moment, those disturbing pale eyes searching hers as if judging her sincerity. It made her curl up with horror inside. "Indeed. Please save a dance for me, Lady Diana." Apparently satisfied, he bowed over her grandmother's hand and, at her cool reception, hastily departed.

Grandmama glanced at Diana as she assisted her from the chair. "Potting houseplants? Flirting as if your life depended on it? I would have refused to believe it if I hadn't witnessed it."

"You must admit Lord Montgomery is quite handsome," Diana murmured, avoiding her gaze.

Her grandmother uttered an inelegant snort. "Yes. If you like the sort. But I would not have thought you would." She narrowed her eyes. "You are up to something," she confirmed with a firm nod, then she took Diana's arm to leave the library. "I only hope it is not dangerous."

"Heavens, no," Diana said breezily. "What a thought."

"You exhaust me, Diana," Grandmama said as they walked toward the stairs. "I will rest for an hour before luncheon."

"I'll assist you up the stairs to your chamber," Diana said, deeply guilt-ridden.

Grandmama patted her arm. "I can manage. I'll come find you." A foot on the step, she glanced back at Diana. "What will you do while I'm resting?"

"I spied some interesting tomes in the library," Diana said. "I'll spend the hour there."

"It appears a harmless means of passing your time, but with you, one never knows." Her worried frown made Diana catch her breath. "Take care, child. There are some here you would not associate with at a London ball."

Diana watched her slowly climb the staircase, disliking causing her grandmother to worry about her. Her warning about the people here had been effective, sending an icy shiver through her. If Lord Montgomery had been the Englishman she'd heard speaking in French near the monument, might she have embarked on something infinitely dangerous? What would Ballantine make of her attention to the viscount? She hoped he'd be jealous.

True to her word, she remained in the library perusing the books until Grandmama reappeared. As they went to the dining room for luncheon, Diana was glad to see the drawn look on her face had gone.

The afternoon passed without incident, and with no sign of Ballantine. During dinner, the Frenchman Monsignor Moreau, seated opposite Diana, mentioned hearing a shot in the gardens when out walking the previous evening. Some said it had woken them. Everyone talked at once. It was decided that it could only have been someone out hunting.

Diana swiveled to catch Ballantine's reaction. He merely drank his wine as the talk flowed around him.

He knew! Had the shot been meant for him? Her blood seemed to run cold in her veins.

As soon as the ladies had left the gentlemen to their port and retired to dress for the ball, Diana hurried upstairs. She must speak to him.

Tims did up the clasps on a ballgown of primrose-colored gauze over a white satin slip, with matching yellow silk slippers. Grandmama sent her lady's maid, Fisher, in to Diana with a delicate diamond pendant and earrings for Diana to wear, and Tims deftly arranged Diana's hair in a flattering style.

"Don't wait up for me, Tims," Diana said as she left her room. "It will be a very late evening."

"Very well, my lady."

"How pretty you look, Diana." In her bedchamber, Grandmama fussed over the powder pot and trinkets on her dressing table. Her powder and familiar lilac perfume filled the air. Diana remembered that scent from when she'd been a small girl; it brought memories of a happier time when her mother had still been with them.

"The diamonds are perfect, Grandmama, thank you." Diana wished she would hurry. She hoped to have words with Ballantine. Perhaps they would dance together.

Her father's smile of approval when she entered the ballroom meant a good deal to her, but only made her feel more guilt-ridden. She thought she'd stopped caring years ago when she'd realized she was a disappointment to him because she was not the son he wished for. But dare she hope his feelings toward her were softening? Some sign of genuine affection? It would not last when she refused yet another suitor, she realized sadly.

Diana eagerly searched the crowded ballroom for Ballantine, wishing to gain his attention, but failed to find him. Lord Montgomery smiled and nodded, and she steeled herself for the difficult evening ahead. Why had she chosen to go down this road, which could end badly for her? She admitted she was impetuous. Her mother had told her so when she'd been small, although Mama had called her "intrepid" when Diana had ridden her pony into the woods without a groom to accompany her. It was true she had never been intimidated by potential consequences.

AFTER A THOROUGH search of the Frenchman Moreau's chamber, Damian came away empty-handed. Even if Moreau were involved in this, his companions had not entrusted the documents to him. It was too large to conceal on his person and extremely difficult to hide it anywhere in Holland House, with the enormous staff attending to every room with scrupulous care. That meant one of the other men still held it in their possession. But who were they? Was Montgomery one of them? His would be the next chamber Damian would search, he decided, as he entered the noisy, brightly lit ballroom where musicians played a country dance by Haydn, and guests danced. As Damian stood watching them, Lady Diana danced into view. In a frothy gown of yellow and white net, she looked a vision. His pleasure at watching how gracefully she moved abruptly ended when her partner turned in the dance to join her. The last man he wished to see anywhere near her. *Montgomery.*

Lady Diana smiled at Damian over Lord Montgomery's shoulder. What the devil was she up to? Was the minx planning something? It wasn't to be borne. But it gave him a chance to search the man's chamber. Damian slipped out through the ballroom doors and hurried toward the staircase.

DIANA'S FATHER SMILED from the edge of the dance floor as she danced with Lord Montgomery. The reverse seemed true of Ballantine, who frowned, his arms folded across his chest as he watched them. It delighted Diana to have stirred some emotion in him. She preferred to believe he was jealous, despite her good sense telling her it was more annoyance when she continued to encourage Lord Montgomery against his advice.

When next Diana looked, the earl had left, and she prayed he had taken advantage of Lord Montgomery's distraction to perform a search of the man's rooms.

As she and Lord Montgomery moved over the floor, she plied him with questions. The sort a woman might have asked a prospective husband. His casual replies were evasive and revealed little about himself. Instead, he turned the conversation back onto her with effusive flattery. Diana considered it a ploy, a means to distract her. It silenced her, fearing he might suspect something more serious lay behind her questions.

"You seem lost in thought, Lady Diana," Lord Montgomery said when the dance brought them together again.

"I am concentrating on the steps, my lord. If you distract me, I shall lose my place."

He laughed. "I don't believe it. You dance divinely." His disturbing eyes searched hers. "May I join you for supper?"

"Certainly, my lord." Diana had already decided she'd learn nothing useful from Lord Montgomery and now that she was sure she had given Ballantine enough time to perform a search of Lord Montgomery's rooms, she needed to extricate herself before it became more difficult. Besides, it would be unseemly to continue dancing with the same gentleman for more than two dances. "I am interested to hear your thoughts on the war. We are all keen observers of Wellesley's successes."

His sandy eyebrows rose. "It will soon come to a glorious end. We must be patient."

"I hope it will be soon. To see Bonaparte vanquished, and England at peace again. What is your opinion of the latest news to reach our shores?"

A tick formed in his jaw. "Ladies ought not concern themselves with the war, Lady Diana."

His answer irritated her, and she fought not to show it. Did she sense a slight cooling in his manner? The war seemed a touchy subject. As the dance ended, she decided Lord Montgomery was far more adept at deception than she was, and she could be right in thinking him a spy.

In the supper room, they filled their plates from the selection of delicious dishes spread over long tables covered in white linen cloths, along with sparkling silverware and fine china dinnerware. Lord Montgomery drew out a chair for her and joined her at a table, while Diana deliberated on how she might proceed. As she cut into a slice of ham, she wondered if Ballantine had searched Lord Montgomery's chamber. He had been absent from the ball for half an hour or more. The sooner she dampened any interest Lord Montgomery might still have in marrying her, the easier it would be.

"But politics interests me greatly, my lord," she said gravely as she sipped her ratafia. "I read the newspapers and periodicals, and confess if I hadn't been born a woman, I would have become a politician." Diana sighed heavily. "How marvelous if one had the power to change things for the better." She leveled a glance at him. "I intend to write pamphlets for any cause I support."

Pushing away his plate of white soup, he narrowed his eyes but merely nodded, and they spent the rest of the meal in relative silence.

ALMOST AN HOUR later, Damian's thorough search had once again proven unsuccessful, and he returned to the ballroom, where dancers performed a gavotte. Other friends soon joined him, and while they stood conversing, he watched Lady Diana's elegant form as she performed the steps. To his relief, she now had a different partner. Damian turned to single out Montgomery and found him standing alone, with a slight, almost proprietorial smile, as he watched Lady Diana. Disquieted, Damian wondered why the man had become so interested in her. It would not be for anything good.

A half hour later, a waltz was called. Damian wasted no time approaching Lady Diana and her grandmother to invite Diana to dance.

Grandmama looked him over with observant eyes, but she permitted it. He offered his arm to the duke's daughter, glad her chaperone appeared aware of the dangers befalling a vulnerable, young woman. But he doubted the older lady could guard her against someone of Montgomery's ilk.

On the dance floor, her deep-blue eyes searched his. "I hoped for a chance to speak to you. The gunshot Monsieur Moreau heard in the garden. Did you hear it too?"

He slipped an arm around her waist. With her hand on his shoulder, and breathing in the sweet scent of roses, he swept her into the waltz. "I saw you dancing with Lord Montgomery."

"That is not an answer," she said sharply. When he glowered

at her and failed to respond, she sighed. "Papa introduced him to me. He's a widower whose wife died several years ago."

So her father considered Montgomery to be a suitor? A heated warning burned through him, tightening his stomach. "How is it that Montgomery has come to your father's notice? Might he be a family friend?"

She shook her head. "I don't believe Papa knows him well."

"You brought this about," he accused her.

"Don't scowl at me." She pursed her lips as she glanced around the room. "People will notice."

"I'd prefer it if you had nothing to do with him, Lady Diana. I suspect he is a dangerous man."

"You left the ballroom. Did you search his room?" she whispered.

He cast her what he hoped was a quelling glance. "Have I said something to make you believe I need to have you as my partner in this?"

Her delightful lips pouted as she frowned. "How ungrateful."

"Lady Diana, I warn you…"

She leaned forward and whispered in his ear. "Was that gunshot meant for you, Ballantine?" Her smile faded. "I couldn't bear it if they shot you."

His heart gave a strange throb when he saw the concern in her eyes. "Why?"

Her lashes lowered. "Because… Because I have a job in mind for you."

It wasn't the answer he'd expected, and he found himself absurdly disappointed. "What kind of job?"

"To help me find my friend, Lady Anne Daintith."

It would prove a fruitless undertaking. At the stark pain darkening her eyes, he struggled with the desire to hold her closer. "After her father paid the ransom and Bow Street made a thorough search," he said, "they concluded she had been killed. They've never found any sign of Lady Anne. It's been months…"

"Only two," she amended angrily, her delicate, arched brows

lowered. "Only a few weeks after it happened, Anne's mother died. Her father, the marquess, has given up looking for her. But I won't. I intend to find her."

He turned her in the dance. "How?" he asked when she came back to him. "You don't know where to look for her."

"I have an idea," she said as the music died away and the waltz came to a close. Dancers around them laughed and chatted as they left the floor. "Can we meet somewhere quiet, away from the guests tomorrow? I shall explain my theory to you."

"I don't see how I can..."

Her eyes implored him. "Please."

"If you promise to stop meddling in my affairs," he said, deciding at least something good might come of it.

"I promise. If I can."

"Make sure you do. I'll meet you by the lake. What time will you be free?"

"When my grandmother takes her nap. I'll come at about one o'clock. Please wait for me."

He clamped his lips down in an attempt to explain how impossible it was. A duke's daughter could hardly go traipsing around the countryside unaccompanied in her search for Lady Anne. He hated seeing Lady Diana distressed by the loss of a close friend, but this idea of hers would lead nowhere.

But even as he thought it, he remembered how strongminded and unshakable she was. To consider the possibility that Lady Anne was alive might distract her from her unhealthy interest in his activities, at least. And he liked the idea of seeing her again.

He bent to whisper in her ear, almost brushing her skin "Will you dance with me again?"

Her cheeks flushed. She nodded her assent, then rested her hand on his arm and he led her from the dance floor.

Dancing with Lady Diana again was fraught with trouble, but he still looked forward to having her in his arms again. Was he in danger of abandoning his long-held conviction that he could not marry while working for the crown? The thought shook him as he rejoined his colleagues. He warned himself to take care. Lady Diana should remain as unapproachable as a star.

"You look to have the weight of the world on your shoulders, Ballantine," Lamb said with a grin. "It must be a lady."

Despite himself, Damian chuckled. Lamb was all too familiar with that problem.

Chapter Nine

WHEN DIANA LEFT the dance floor, her heart raced. His warm breath stirring her hair and the promise of another dance sent a thrill through her. Had he changed his mind? Was that glimmer of hope that he might agree to help her foolish?

"I see you enjoyed your dance with Lord Ballantine," Grandmama observed when Diana sat beside her.

"He has asked me to dance again."

Her grandmother's smile was one of relief. "Then you are not drawn to Viscount Montgomery."

"Lord Ballantine is not the marrying kind, they say."

"Don't most men say that?"

Diana giggled. "Well, I don't wish to marry Lord Montgomery, Grandmama."

"I am relieved to hear it," Grandmama said.

"Why did you take a set against him?"

"It was mere instinct. But I found a lack of warmth in his eyes and thought his manner forced." She patted Diana's hand. "I shall try to convince your father that he won't do."

Thankful for her support, Diana smiled. "I would be grateful if you could, Grandmama."

"Well, you were herding his thoughts in that direction as a collie dog herds sheep, dear girl. But I shall see what I can do."

Diana searched for Ballantine and found him engaged in

conversation with an elegant woman she hadn't met. They were laughing together. A swift rush of jealousy heated her cheeks, dismaying her. Did he flirt with all the women? When he flirted with her, did it meant nothing?

It was important not to allow her emotions to become involved if she was to elicit his help. Still, she couldn't help wondering what her grandmother thought of Ballantine. "What does your insight tell you about Lord Ballantine, Grandmama?"

Her grandmother's gaze followed Diana's to where he stood. "Handsome in a lean, rugged way. Not pretty, like Lord Montgomery. I like his firm chin. But there is something elusive about the earl. I've heard nothing detrimental. Ballantine's country estate is in Berkshire. The mansion is a fine example of Elizabethan architecture, I believe. He has no living parents, but a brother. They lost their sister many years ago." She turned to look at Diana. "Perhaps it is that unknowable quality which intrigues you, child. As well as his fine physique, of course."

Diana was about to deny it when, at the announcement of the last dance of the evening, Ballantine left his companion and crossed the floor to claim her, making her heart jump.

"It appears he also has you on his mind, Diana," Grandmama said thoughtfully. "Perhaps I should give him more of my attention."

She silently groaned. It wouldn't be long before her grandmother became aware there was something between Diana and Ballantine. She must be careful. But there wasn't much between her and Ballantine to keep from her grandmother, for theirs wasn't a romance. Was it?

The country dance made conversation difficult. Although it didn't prevent Ballantine from warning her against Lord Montgomery, again, as they stood together waiting for the rest of dancers to enter the dance floor.

He looked subdued, his demeanor very different to how he'd been during their last dance. She wasn't sure why he'd changed, but it disappointed her. "I can think for myself, sir," she protested.

"And have already decided there is nothing I can do to help in that regard."

His alert, brown eyes searched her face, as if reassuring himself it was true. "I'm relieved to hear it."

"Did you find anything incriminating?" she couldn't help asking when the steps brought them together.

He raised a dark eyebrow. "Where?"

"When you went to search his chamber," she said, out of all patience with him.

"How well yellow suits you, Lady Diana," Ballantine said, raising his voice above the din.

She glared at him.

"Was my compliment not to your taste?" he asked, lifting his eyebrows.

"The color is called primrose. You meant to distract me. I am not so easily fooled, my lord."

He cocked his head and smiled slightly. "It was sincerely meant. You look like a fragrant flower."

Warmth spread up her neck, and she feared she had a silly smile on her face. "We shall dispense with this nonsense when we talk tomorrow," she dared to whisper when they came together again.

"Shall we? Pity. I enjoy praising a pretty woman and having her in my arms."

She felt the flush deepen on her cheeks. He had not bothered to lower his voice. A lady in their set overheard them and giggled.

Diana's face still burned when Ballantine returned her to her chair.

He wasn't a man to be manipulated. She suddenly felt very dispirited. Her plan to find Anne suddenly seemed unlikely to succeed. "Shall we go up to bed, Grandmama? I am rather tired."

Grandmama observed her but blessedly asked no questions.

As Diana settled into bed and blew out the candle, she went over the evening in her mind. She believed that her dance with Lord Montgomery had allowed Ballantine to search the viscount's chamber. Why else would he be away from the ballroom for so long? But of course, he would continue to deny it.

She prayed Grandmama could successfully quash her father's interest in Lord Montgomery. But there was something about the way he had looked at her when she'd rattled on about politics and spoke of a desire to write pamphlets. A steely expression had come into his eyes, as if he saw through her, which made her swallow nervously. He was not a man to dupe, and she feared could be dangerous if she persisted.

⋙✦⋘

AFTER ANOTHER HEADY dance with Lady Diana, where Damian sought, somewhat unsuccessfully, to cool things down, he did at last manage to gain some discipline over his thoughts and concentrate on the reason he had been sent here.

Since nothing had been found in Montgomery's room, he made his last attempt to locate the documents by searching the chamber allotted to the Frenchman Jean-Claude de La Touche, a man who had ingratiated himself into English society by employing his knowledge of the French to good use. Damian's opportunity came after breakfast the next morning, when he spied, through a window, the man leaving in a hackney as Damian was about to climb the stairs.

"Where has Monsignor gone?" he asked a footman at the door. "I wished to speak to him."

"I heard him direct the jarvie to the docks, my lord."

So the Frenchman was arranging his passage to France. Damian ran up the stairs. Would he have taken the documents with him? It was unlikely when the chance of being robbed rose considerably in the area around the docks.

De La Touche's bedchamber was on the second floor at the rear of the building. Damian entered the empty room, then stood and took stock. The Frenchman had neatly ordered his possessions, lining up his brush and comb on the dresser, and Damian intended to leave the chamber exactly as he'd found it after making a thorough search. He opened the bureau drawers, which contained folded cravats, stockings, and laundered shirts. Nothing beneath the mattress. Opening the wardrobe door, Damian checked the pockets of de La Touche's spare tailcoat, his evening clothes and banyan hanging on a hook. Although the man would be gone for a while, Damian didn't want a maid to come in and find him here. Nor did he want the occupants of the neighboring rooms becoming interested.

He stepped back and looked around. If he wished to hide documents here, where would he put them so servants wouldn't accidentally come across them?

He flipped back the edges of the rug, then straightened, empty-handed. Not there. Turning to the bed, he pulled back the covers and sheets and removed the pillowslips from the pillows. He ran his hand over the squabs of a chair upholstered in dark-blue velvet. Something rustled. His pulse racing, Damian plunged his hand up inside the loose slip cover. His fingers touched paper. He drew out a document and unfolded it. With no doubt, this was one of the two stolen documents that his spymaster had sent him to find.

"Not a very imaginative hiding place, de La Touche," Damian murmured. "But thank you."

When his search failed to turn up the other document, he smoothed the chair covers and replaced the linen on the bed. Then he checked the room to be sure he'd left no sign of his search before tucking the paper inside his coat. He cautiously opened the door. The corridor was empty, but when he headed for the stairs, a door opened farther down the hall.

Montgomery stepped out. "Calling on someone, Ballantine?" he asked with his humorless smile.

"A gentleman never tells, Montgomery." Damian walked past him.

Leaving the man watching him, he ran down the stairs. He

must pass this document on to Scovell before the spies wrestled it back from him. Damian didn't doubt they'd use force.

Leaving the house, he hurried along the drive to the stables and requested a groom saddle a horse. Mounting, he rode toward the gates. As he grew close, a gunshot broke the silence. Damian felt a sharp pain high on his arm. He gritted his teeth and galloped on.

By the time he'd reached the Horse Guards in London, blood dripped down from the gunshot wound on his right arm onto his hand. He dismounted, tossed the reins to a soldier on duty, and, wiping his fingers with a handkerchief, ran into the building. He knocked, then flung open the door at Scovell's invitation. Taking a few steps across the floor toward the startled man seated at the desk, Damian stopped to wipe the blood from his fingers with his handkerchief before it dripped on the carpet.

Scovell threw back his chair and rose, coming around the desk. "What the devil has happened, Ballantine?"

"Someone took exception to me leaving Holland House with this in my possession. They winged me." Damian pulled the document from the pocket of his coat, winced, and handed it to his spymaster.

Scovell opened it out on the desk. "Good man. I'll send for the surgeon. You've done what I trusted you'd do. Take a well-earned rest until that arm heals." He went to the cabinet and poured two glasses of brandy, handing one to Damian.

Glad of it, Damian tossed it down. "I need to get back to Holland House. This is little more than a graze. A bandage will suffice."

The brandy took the edge off the pain. Damian eased himself out of his ruined coat and shirt. The ball had caused a deep furrow in the muscle before it had exited. Thankfully, it didn't require stitching.

After the summoned doctor had patched Damian and left them, Scovell questioned him. "Can you give me their names?"

"Only de La Touche. I suspect Viscount Montgomery is

involved. Has he had access to the war office?"

Scovell looked grim. "Once. Came in with a Lord Williams." He held up a hand. "Williams is one hundred percent trustworthy."

"Charles Moreau may be the third spy. I have no other suspect to offer. But I lack any definitive proof for either of these men."

"What about Holland?"

"It's common knowledge that he and Lady Holland support Bonaparte, but I've seen no evidence to think it goes further."

"That's it, then," Scovell said. "Do not go back there. You could walk into a trap."

While he agreed that was certainly possible, he had promised to meet Lady Diana. He wasn't about to let her down.

It was past one o'clock when Damian arrived back at Holland House in a fresh shirt, cravat, and coat, supplied by Scovell's office to replace his ruined clothes. His pistol was loaded and tucked into the back of his breeches. He kept a wary eye out for any sign of a disturbance in the gardens. Perhaps they didn't expect him back. Maybe they feared the game was up, for no one approached him or took a shot at him.

He left the horse at the stables, expecting Lady Diana to have given up on him. In case she hadn't, he made his way to the lake.

She was still there, throwing some cabbage leaves to the ducks. Seeing him, she came to meet him. "I thought you weren't coming. Grandmama will be downstairs at two o'clock." She placed a hand on his arm, making him pull away with a wince.

Her eyes widened. "What is wrong? Have you hurt your arm?"

"A touch of rheumatism," Damian said with an amused smile. His gaze swept the scene as he held her elbow and drew her away from the noisy ducks flocking around her on the bank. He led her into the summerhouse, which offered a measure of shelter and a good view of the surrounding meadows beyond the lake, should anyone come by. He intended to deal with this quickly, as she would be in danger if seen with him.

Once within the wooden-framed dwelling, he felt the full force of Lady Diana's searching blue eyes. "You're hurt, Ballantine. What happened?"

"It's nothing." He casually folded his arms then tightened his lips on a grunt as pain shot through him. "We're here to discuss your problem. And we have little time in which to do it," he said, hoping to hurry her and return her safe to the house.

"Well, yes. As I told you, I want you to help me find my friend, Lady Anne Daintith."

He gazed at her warily. "You must at least consider that after all this time, your friend no longer lives."

She raised her chin. "I am not yet prepared to believe that."

"But where can you even begin to look for her?"

"When Lord Daintith held a memorial for Anne at Daintith Park, I questioned the coachman. He told me exactly where the kidnapper held up the Daintith carriage and abducted her, but not where her father left the ransom for them to pick up. It was an inn and could not have been far, as Lord Daintith rode there and back in the same day." She paused to take a deep breath. "So you see, the two events are less than twenty miles apart, which could mean the rogue is somewhere in that area. If we were to search the villages and surrounding countryside, we might discover where he keeps her."

It was pitifully inadequate. He reached up and stroked a finger over her trembling chin. "What reason would he have to keep her alive?" he asked gently.

Her shoulders slumped, and she covered her face with her hands. "I don't know."

He held her shaking shoulders, wishing he could draw her into his arms. "You believe your father will let you traipse around the countryside with me looking for her?"

She drew away and gazed up at him, blinking away tears. "No, of course he won't. My father and grandmother attended the memorial. They don't share my opinion that Anne still lives. I shall have to keep it from them both. I don't like to, but I am prepared to do it, for Anne's sake."

Ballantine heard a rustle and cast around for movement in the gardens. When nothing moved, he turned back to her. "I fear it would be a wild goose chase. But if you wish it, I will make a thorough search of the area."

"We shall go together." Her lovely eyes filled with hope. "I intend to tell Papa I am visiting a friend in Bath for a sennight. He is about to begin a new painting and will let me go without questioning me."

He frowned at her. "And if something happens to you during this foolish quest? What am I to tell him?"

"He will know nothing about you."

"You think I would be low enough to hide the truth from him?"

She placed a hand on his good arm and gazed appealingly into his face. "No, of course I don't. Do this for me, Ballantine. I have a very strong feeling. An instinct, my grandmother calls it. Anne still lives. I cannot explain it. We have been close friends forever."

He nodded. "I believe one can sense when loved ones are in danger or have passed away. Perhaps that applies to friends, too." He had felt strongly that his colleague, Joshua Blackson, had walked into a trap when they'd been on a mission in France. But he had arrived too late to save him. The loss of Blackson had left him disillusioned and determined for it never to happen again. While he refused to place Lady Diana in danger, he didn't want her to feel she had failed her friend.

"Very well," he said, wondering if he'd lost his mind. "If, and it's a big 'if,' you can meet me without your father discovering it, I shall help you."

Should the duke learn of it, he would assume it was an elopement. They would then have to marry. It brought him up short. His plan not to marry until he gave up his work still stood. But now Lady Diana was determined to go and nothing would stop her.

"I'll write to my friend in Bath. Penny sends frequent letters to invite me to visit. When Papa and I return to Ashburnham House after we leave here, I shall send her a letter asking her if I might stay. Her mother is always pleased to see me. Then I'll meet you somewhere of your choosing on the Bath road."

"Yes, but will she keep your secret?"

"Penny is a dear friend. We have always kept each other's secrets. During our first London Season, we relied on each other a good deal."

"She hasn't married?"

"No, her betrothed died while away fighting on the Peninsula."

"Very well." Not displeased by the thought of seeing her again, he still feared this adventure could go badly wrong. And for what? Her friend Lady Anne must have been dead. For what kidnappers kept the evidence of their crime alive to alert the magistrate and send them to the gallows?

"I must go back to the house," she said. "Grandmama will wonder where I am."

He drew his calling card from his wallet, which bore both his addresses. "Write to me at my country address. When we next meet, you can share with me all that you know about Lady Anne, her family, and your beliefs regarding the abduction's location and where the ransom was left."

De La Touche might have returned and reported the missing document to the other two men. It was time for Damian to leave.

"Return to the house," he said. "We shall not speak until we meet again."

Her gaze roamed his face. "Something bad has occurred, Ballantine. You've hurt your arm…and I saw you ride away from Holland House. I waited for you. I had faith you'd come back. Where did you go? Will you tell me what happened?"

"If you wish me to help you, don't persist, please." He pushed her gently. "Now go."

She paused on the path to look back at him, her eyes dark with worry, then hurried away.

Chapter Ten

DIANA ENTERED THE house, breathless after a mad dash along the garden paths. Her grandmother hovered in the corridor outside the dining room, frowning.

"Where have you been? They are about to serve refreshments."

"I went for a walk."

Grandmama raised her brows. "In the woods? Your hair is coming down and burrs have attached themselves to your skirt."

Diana tucked a loose curl behind her ear. "I left the path for a better view of the lake. It's very picturesque. Cook gave me some vegetable scraps for the ducks."

Grandmama furrowed her eyebrows. "Run upstairs, tidy your hair, and change your gown. I shall wait for you in the drawing room."

"Yes, Grandmama," Diana said meekly. *Drat!* She looked at the prickles on her hem. The few gowns she had with her had become crushed and needed ironing. About to climb the staircase, she glanced through the long window and saw Ballantine carrying a portmanteau, climbing into a hackney with his valet. He was leaving Holland House again. Knowing she wouldn't see him again for several weeks, she put a hand to her chest, which felt strangely hollow.

She hurried up the stairs, intent on finding something suitable to wear, and failed to see the man standing on the gloomy landing until she almost walked into him.

Lord Montgomery seized her arms, supposedly to steady her, but his fingers dug into her skin. "What has caused this head-long dash, Lady Diana?"

Unnerved, she stepped back from him. "I require a change of gown, sir, and I'm in dire need of a cool drink."

He studied her, his gaze pausing on the spot of mud on her skirt. "You seem to have enjoyed your time in the gardens."

He made it sound as if she'd been romping about in the grass. She raised her chin. "I found it pleasant to be out on such a nice day."

"I imagine it was. Many ladies would relish a clandestine meeting with that rake, the Earl of Ballantine."

Had he been watching her? She teased her bottom lip with her teeth as she considered her reply. "Hardly that. I happened upon him when I went to feed the waterfowl. If you'll excuse me, my grandmother is waiting for me."

She moved to brush past him, but he stepped in her way, his eyes narrowed. "It isn't easy to fool me, Lady Diana."

As this confirmed her own opinion of him, a prickle of alarm gripped her stomach. She forced a laugh. "I don't know to what you refer, my lord."

His jaw tightened. "You would not want me to go to your father with the sordid truth of your behavior. He would dislike hearing how you lied to him and how you toyed with a man's affections."

Diana frowned. She had to admit she was partly guilty. "My father would not be swayed by anything you might tell him, Lord Montgomery. He is more than capable of making up his own mind. He is a man of considerable intellect."

"You encouraged your father to introduce us, did you not? And gave him the impression you would consider our marriage."

As she could hardly refute it, she kept silent.

"But were you ever interested in marrying me?" His cruel

eyes studied her. "Or was I a mere foil to distract your father while you carried on with your lover, a man of mystery you know the duke will never accept? Should Ballantine even wish for your hand? I doubt it's marriage he has on his mind." He shook his head. "He has a shadowy past and moves in less-than-exalted circles. I admit to being dumbfounded by your choice to associate with such a deplorable rake. And I am more than a little annoyed to have been used."

He seemed to loom over her, his eyes now a stormy charcoal gray. She swallowed, nerves tightening her throat. He must have been watching from the bushes, but who had piqued his interest? Was it her or Ballantine? Did he *know* Ballantine was a spy? Wishing to extricate herself, she glanced around, hoping for a servant to appear. "I don't know what you mean, Lord Montgomery. Lord Ballantine is not, nor has he ever been, my lover. It's absurd to suggest such a thing. And it is insulting."

"There is no use lying to me. I saw you two alone together in the summerhouse."

"For the briefest moment. We discussed the Earl of Elgin's recent acquisition and how we would like to view the marbles when they display them for the public."

"Don't pull the wool over my eyes! There was more going on between you. I thought it a touching scene between two people on very familiar terms with each other."

She gaped at him. "That's nonsense."

"You deny it?"

"Yes, of course I do. If you go to my father with this falsehood, I shall tell him you have behaved in a disgraceful manner toward me." She tried to dodge around him.

But he stopped her again, the anger fading from his eyes to be replaced with dismay. "I see I have been unfair. Please accept my apology, Lady Diana. I believe it was jealousy that made me behave so badly. I am not myself. I hope you will forgive me."

Diana didn't believe him. She thought that everything he did and said was calculated. And she just wanted to be free of him.

"Then we shall forget it happened," she said, escaping to her bedchamber.

Safely inside, she locked the door and leaned back against it, gasping. Tims looked up from ironing the blue muslin, concern in her eyes. "Are you all right, my lady?"

Diana put a hand to her chest. "Oh, yes. I ran up the stairs too fast." How much she missed Ballantine's protection already! Lord Montgomery had behaved like a spurned lover. But she struggled to believe he really was one. He'd tried to manipulate her and when his blustering hadn't worked, he'd tried another tactic. Would he carry out his threat and cause trouble between her and Papa? She trembled at the uproar which would follow. Her father would bar her from leaving the estate for months and she'd miss the opportunity to search for Anne with Ballantine. A distressed, angry sob rose in her throat.

After changing, she took the time to compose herself, placing a cool washcloth against her hot cheeks before going downstairs. Smoothing her pale-blue muslin trimmed with lemon ribbon, a matching ribbon her maid had threaded through her curls, she entered through the drawing room door a servant had opened for her to be greeted with laughter, chatter, the smell of fresh baked bread, and the clink of crockery.

Grandmama acknowledged her dress with an approving nod and patted the place beside her, then continued her conversation with the lady seated on the sofa to her left. Diana crossed the carpet and joined them as the footmen and maids moved around the room serving bread and butter, cold meat, cake, fruit, tea, wine, and lemonade.

Her father entered, appearing quite calm. Diana dragged in a relieved breath. Lord Montgomery hadn't sought him out. Had the viscount merely said those things to try to stir her sympathy? He didn't love her, that was nonsense. She sensed something more serious lay behind his actions than anything she might have done. After all, they had only shared one dance. Was their marriage of great importance to him? Did he need the backing of a family such as theirs? His ungentlemanly behavior, especially when she was a young, unmarried woman, astonished her and she suspected, had been uncharacteristic of him. She believed him to be a sly and cautious man. Something had made him furious.

Was what he'd told her about Ballantine true? She was already convinced he was a spy. But a rake? If he were, Grandmama would have heard about it. No juicy gossip ever escaped her or her dowager friends. If it was true, she thought Ballantine would make a very poor sort of rake. Apart from the kiss, which seemed to have affected him as much as it had her, he had resisted every opportunity to seduce her.

She remembered what Lord Montgomery had said about the touching scene between her and Ballantine. Could there be something unspoken and as yet unacknowledged between them? She had tried not to think that way about him, although it was difficult, especially at night, alone with her thoughts. But he was only protective of her. She liked that quality in a man, but it left her wishing for more.

They were to meet again, and she remained hopeful the romantic liaison to which Lord Montgomery had referred might become a reality. Lord Montgomery's words had shocked her because it forced her to admit she was that disgraceful person he accused her of being, at least at heart. Diana sat rigid in the seat, her hands clasped demurely in her lap. She could almost sense Grandmama beside her assessing her mood. Especially when she glanced at her. But blessedly, she made no comment, even though Diana feared her crimson cheeks gave her away. Would she question Diana later? She disliked having to lie to Grandmama, whom she loved dearly. Thoroughly unsettled, she took a glass of lemonade and a plate of iced cake from a footman, then turned to join in the conversation beside her as if she hadn't a worry in the world.

ON RETURNING TO Scovell's office, the men crowded around and slapped Damian on the back. Once the document reached Wellesley, the general would have vital information in his possession that could change the outcome of his next campaign. But there was still one document missing.

Therefore, Scovell expressed some disappointment at not having definitively discerned the identity of the other two spies, or found the other document, but they had arrested de La Touche before he could board a ship and the Frenchman would be persuaded to give up their names. As Viscount Montgomery, and Monsieur Charles Moreau remained suspects, they would be closely watched while they were in London.

Damian had already decided to lie low at his country estate for a few weeks, and he agreed with Scovell that returning to Holland House would be reckless.

As he entered his Mayfair townhouse, his thoughts returned to his meeting with Lady Diana. He hoped no one had seen them alone together at the lake. Gossip would quickly spread, especially in such a cloistered environment as Holland House. Her father would demand an explanation. And Damian had no satisfactory justification for spending time alone with the duke's daughter. Fathers tended to believe the worst. And usually, they were right. He could hardly tell Ashburnham his daughter was determined to rescue her friend, Lady Anne, and considered Damian the means to bring it about. If the duke forced his hand and insisted they marry, Damian would be in the very devil of a pickle, especially with Scovell considering sending him to France after a month's respite.

If he were in a position to consider marriage, Lady Diana would be the lady he would choose to be captured in the parson's mousetrap. She was everything he wished for in a wife: bold and brave, sensitive, sympathetic, and utterly gorgeous. The bond between them was so strong, he struggled to ignore it. But he would not give up his important work, and to leave her alone for months on end, she not knowing if he was alive or dead, was too heartless to contemplate. Apart from the babes who might ensue from their union. He couldn't help smiling at that. He wasn't averse to children and relished the thought of having the lady in his bed, but no, he couldn't marry her.

In the morning, with his valet seated alongside him, Damian drove his curricle out of London on his way to Longview Hall, his Berkshire estate. Time spent in the country always served to renew his energy. He enjoyed seeing his younger brother, Luke, of whom he was most fond, discussing estate matters with him and his bailiff, and riding over his acres to visit the tenants.

Luke had lived with Damian for two years since his manor house had burned down and he'd lost his beloved wife, Marianne, in the fire. The tragedy had occurred after a servant had upturned a branch of candles near the parlor curtains. Fire had quickly spread to the upper stories, trapping Marianne. They had been married for seven months and she'd been carrying his child.

Fearing Luke was grieving too deeply, Damian had invited him to move into Longview Hall and take over the running of the estate while he was away. At least until Luke felt up to returning to restoring his house, a handsome property he had inherited from one of their aunts.

The sky had darkened to deep violet by the time he drove his horses through the gates and continued along the arrow-straight drive through acres of green sward toward Longview Hall and into the ancient trees of the park. An obliging hunter's moon shone down to light his way. The house loomed, the pale stone glowing richly except for where ivy grew over the walls of the east wing. Candlelight shone out from the long windows in the hall as Damian guided his tired horses around to the stable block.

Once the groom attended to his horses, Damian walked along the gravel drive to the southern front of the house, pulling off his gloves. Tired and hungry, he yawned. Having left London at dawn, the day had been long and the intermittent rain showers tedious. He'd stopped only to rest the horses and grab a bite of luncheon.

Reaching the front, he found Barron, his butler and his father's before him, standing at the open door throwing a welcome arc of light out into the dark. Damian entered and greeted him, handing him his hat and gloves. "Are you well, Barron?"

"I am indeed. Thank you, my lord."

"Is Mr. Beaufort in the library?"

"He is, my lord."

"I'll take supper there. Anything the cook has on hand, Barron."

As Damian walked along the corridor, his red setter, Max ran to meet him.

"How are you, fella?" Damian said, crouching down and stroking the dog's silky head.

Luke always sought the library in the evenings. He'd sit by the fire and read. Apparently, it helped him sleep. Damian had other ideas about that but kept it to himself. No sense in prodding his brother to pick up the threads of his life. Luke would seek feminine company again when the time was right.

He opened the library door and Max scampered ahead to stretch out on the rug. Damian's brother rose from a chair and placed his book on the table. He crossed the Persian rugs to draw Damian into a hug. "You didn't send a message that you were coming. I feared our dreaded aunts had taken it upon themselves to visit unannounced."

Damian chuckled. "The last time I saw her, Aunt Hattie was happily ensconced in Bath society. I don't expect Aunt Amy would call on her own. Her older sister is always the instigator."

Luke's half-smile was gloomy. "Aunt Hattie sends me letters encouraging me to marry again. Nothing I say deters her, so I've given up trying."

"I suspect she considers me a lost cause."

"I doubt it," Luke said with a laugh. "Once you turn thirty, it will renew their interest."

Damian dropped into his favorite highbacked wingchair and propped his boots on the low table. He studied his brother, disappointed to find Luke's blue eyes, very like their mother's, still held a haunted cast. But his face was less gaunt, and his big frame had filled out, and he appeared well muscled from working about the land.

Luke poured two brandies from a crystal decanter and came to hand one to him. "I am always overjoyed to see you. Never know if I'll get bad news."

"I hate you worrying about me." The long drive had stirred up his wound and his arm ached where the ball had scored the flesh. Damian took a good, long swallow of the excellent brandy from his cellar, some bottles brought back from France on his last trip there.

Luke swiped back his dark hair. "We do what we must."

"I promise to settle down one day."

His brother raised his eyebrows. "Is there a lady who might tempt you?"

Damian sighed. He would like to tell Luke about Lady Diana and how utterly fascinating she was, but that would only give his brother false hope. "Not while there's important work to be done."

Luke rose to stab the glowing coals with the poker. Sparks flew up the chimney. "Then I expect I shall go on worrying."

"How did the spring planting go? Have enough seasonal workers?" Damian asked to distract him.

A servant brought in a tray with a warm meat pie that flavored the air and placed it, as well as a small dish of sauce, some cheese and pickle, and a pile of bread and butter before him. As Damian ate, Luke spoke about yields, the recent work undertaken, and the latest happenings in the village. Damian was glad to see his brother's eyes had brightened. He would spend the next few weeks here with Luke, until summoned by Lady Diana, and hoped to find his brother even more eager to embrace his future when he returned.

Chapter Eleven

ASHBURNHAM HOUSE SETTLED into its usual routine. Grandmama had returned to her townhouse in London to see friends before it grew too hot, and Papa began a new painting. When Diana met him at dinner, once he'd enquired after her day, he became lost in his thoughts while gazing at her speculatively. Was he considering another husband for her? Although his standards were high, so far, those he'd chosen had failed to suit her, which made her nervous. She relied on his usual disinterest when she must broach the subject of her visit to Penny.

Diana hadn't yet received a reply from Penny. She dealt with her impatience by riding over the meadows until Artemis was ready for her stall, and she was a little calmer.

Five days later, their butler, Burrows, handed Diana the post with a smile as she hovered in the hall. The letter had come from Bath. Two pages, crossed and crammed into every available space. The postage would be expensive. Heart beating fast, Diana hurried upstairs to read it.

How absolutely intriguing! Penny wrote. *An adventure! Is the earl very handsome? I am guessing he is! Of course you may come a little later than expected. I shall find an excuse to satisfy Mama. I love intrigues! If only I could play a bigger part in it. But I have met someone, Diana!* A paragraph followed, describing the paragon Penny loved desperately. *He is so very charming. It's too early to tell, but I am hopeful we might suit.*

Diana turned the paper on its side to read the last few lines. *I pray you find Anne, the sweetest person you could ever meet. She, of all people, did not deserve such a horrid fate. I hope you bring good news when you arrive. Even the smallest suspicion that she might still live. Shall I have a glimpse of your handsome protector? I am consumed with curiosity, and I can't wait to see you.*

At her desk, Diana took out a sheet of bond. She would write to convey her delight at Penny's news and her promise to tell her all when they met, if there was much to tell. But first, she must write to Ballantine. She took out the card he had given her with his estate and Mayfair addresses, tucked into her glove drawer. As she dipped her quill in the inkpot, excitement rose in her chest like bubbles of champagne. Finally, she could search for Anne. She could read the doubt in Penny's words, but Diana refused to consider the possibility her friend, Anne, would never be found. It was too painful. She would ensure this letter went off in the next post and then must wait for Ballantine's reply. She had written that she'd been unable to locate the Hare and Hounds Inn and relied on him to do so.

In her letter, she described Anne's home in Chippenham, and the woodland where the kidnapping had taken place. She described the location where the coach had been held up, which was not a great distance from Anne's home. The inn could not be more than a half day's ride away. *So, as you see, it all occurred within a relatively small area. I know you will say it made it expedient for a quick escape, but what if there's another reason? What if the rogue has a property in the vicinity? Even Bristol is not very far away, especially if they traveled by the back roads.*

She signed it, put down her pen, and blotted the paper, hoping she'd made an excellent case for Ballantine to take up her cause. He wouldn't refuse her now, would he?

After another agonizing wait of almost a week, Ballantine's letter arrived. Diana snatched it up from the silver salver in the hall and whisked it away before it came to her father's notice. Closing her bedroom door, she sat at her desk and broke the seal.

She unfolded the page with trembling fingers.

It was a brisk letter, merely signed with his title. As her coachman would take her to Bath, Ballantine wrote, he would take her and her maid up in his carriage in Milsom Street near the corner of Green Street, the day of her arrival, which he trusted would be Monday next, at one o'clock. If something occurred to prevent her, she was to send a message to Longview Hall.

She considered Milsom Street a good choice. It wasn't far from the Howards' townhouse. She could walk there when she returned to Bath. The coachman would accept her excuse that she needed to do some last-minute shopping. The street was always crowded with shoppers and visitors to the town. She would have to pack lightly in a portmanteau she could carry herself; otherwise, their driver, Horace, would insist on delivering her luggage to Penny's house.

Diana turned her attention to her clothes while wrestling with another problem. Her lady's maid fussed around the bedchamber, helping her select what to take. Diana could not have her involved. She gazed at the slim, red-haired girl who carefully folded a spencer. "Tims, would you like to visit your mother while I'm in Bath?"

"I would, my lady," Tims said with a grin.

"The coach will drop you there on my way to Bath, and I'll pick you up again later. But don't mention it to the staff, will you?" She laughed. "Or everyone will want the same."

Tims's freckled face grew serious. "I won't say a word, my lady."

"I know I can rely on you, Tims. I'll take the blue muslin," Diana said, pleased the issue of her maid had been easy to take care of. Tims wouldn't tell—she was too wary of Grandmama.

Diana could only be grateful her grandmother had not returned from London to the dower house, where she could be called upon to accompany Diana to Bath.

She pulled out her cape, smiling at the thought of what lay ahead. Days spent in Ballantine's company, and finding Anne and freeing her from her abductor. Did he hold her in the hope that more money might be forthcoming?

⤜⤜⤜✦⤛⤛⤛

DAMIAN SPENT THE evening in the library after dinner, explaining to his bemused brother why he must dash off to Bath.

"Is it a lady?" Luke asked again.

"A lady in distress, you might say," Damian conceded.

"Aha!"

"You can create all manner of attractive scenarios, Luke, but I shall not return engaged."

"How long will this…gallant undertaking of yours take? Will I expect you back this month?"

"Only a week at most."

After a day, or two at the most, Damian would drive back to Bath and deliver Lady Diana to her friend's home. That would be the limit to his endurance. Putting up overnight at an inn would prove incredibly difficult to keep Lady Diana's reputation intact, not to mention the strain on his self-control. He admitted he had humored her, believing this a lost cause. But she was a game girl. If he didn't take her, she'd attempt it with someone else, or worse, alone. And if something bad happened to her, he'd never forgive himself.

At the sideboard, Luke sighed. "At least this doesn't sound dangerous." He poured them both a cognac. "Well, not life-threatening."

Damian smiled as he took it. He swirled the golden liquid in the balloon glass. "Nothing like it. I would tell you the whole, but discretion…"

Luke nodded. "Is the better part of valor? I agree with the bard."

"I'd trust you with my life, Luke, and might one day have the lady's consent to tell you all of it." Perhaps Lady Diana wouldn't object, but revealing his plan to Luke would either result in setting the fox among the chickens when he'd advise him of not undertaking something so rash, or have his brother chortling over Damian's dashed foolishness. And he would agree with him.

Luke raised his glass. "I must admit, I'm intrigued. You excel at getting yourself out of tricky situations, but maybe you'll meet your match with the lady."

Damian shook his head. "Not until the end of this infernal war, and I'm ready to wed."

"I'll see you off in the morning."

"A game of chess or billiards before we retire?"

"Billiards," Luke said quickly. "A farmer needs his sleep, and I can defeat you faster at that than chess."

Damian cocked an eyebrow, then laughed. "You're on."

The next morning after breakfast, Damian traveled to Bath in his brother's carriage. He rested his feet on the opposite seat, folded his arms, and fought boredom. He disliked coach travel and avoided it where he could, much preferring to ride or drive his curricle. Damian's coach with the crest on the door panel would alert people to who he was and stir up considerable interest. And that was the last thing he wanted.

It was close to one o'clock when the carriage entered Bath and drove down Milsom street. Damian watched the busy thoroughfare while searching for a familiar slim figure. Approaching Green Street, there she was, huddled in a hooded cape and clutching a portmanteau. A little amused, he tapped on the roof with his cane, and they pulled up beside her. Lady Diana saw the carriage and hurried over, pleased to see him. She seemed to relish an adventure and this chance to discover news of Lady Anne. He would hate to see her disappointed.

When his groom escorted her inside the carriage, Damian breathed in her scent as he lowered the blinds. When Damian turned back to her, his heart gave a leap at her lovely face, her dark-blue eyes wide, her delectable lips slightly open. Eager for adventure. *Dear Lord, give me strength*, he silently prayed. "Where is your maid?"

"I left Tims at her parents' house in Combe Down. I must fetch her before I return to Bath. A slight detour. Will that be all right?"

He nodded, uneasy about having Lady Diana to himself. While it was pleasurable, it was also dangerous. "Your father was happy for you to make the journey?"

"Yes." Lady Diana pushed back the hood of her green cape and undid the frog fastenings, easing it off her shoulders. She wore a pale gray carriage gown beneath it, the high neck trimmed with lace. Putting the cape aside, she pulled off her gloves. "But a visitor called just as I was leaving…"

Her pause made him wary. He raised his eyebrows. "Who?"

"It was Lord Montgomery. He came to see Papa."

"Montgomery?" Apprehension and an annoying stab of jealousy ratcheted through him. "What would he want with your father? Did he come to claim your hand?"

"No," she blurted out. "I made sure he understood I wasn't interested. But, Ballantine…" She sat forward on the seat. "He saw us together in the summerhouse and threatened to tell Papa. I fear that might be his aim."

"That was unfortunate," he murmured. Was all about to come crashing down on their heads? By Montgomery? He wouldn't trust the fellow an inch. But would he have another reason to call on the duke?

"I should take you to Miss Howard's townhouse and leave you there," he said, biting off a curse.

Lady Diana looked horrified. "Oh, no, please don't, Ballantine. Even should Lord Montgomery reveal what he saw, and even if he should embellish it, there's no reason for Papa to come to Bath and remove me from the Howards'." She reached over and slipped her slim, warm hand in his. "If we don't find Anne soon, it will be too late. I cannot let her down."

It was unwise to continue, but her pleading gaze was his undoing. He supposed if Montgomery carried out his threat and this mad escapade fell apart, angering her father, it hardly mattered if they continued on their quest or not.

He gazed down at that small, gloved hand and gave it a slight squeeze, releasing it. "If we uncover nothing by tomorrow afternoon, I'll take you to the Howards."

Her eyes brightened. "Well, what are we waiting for?"

Damian instructed his coachman as to their direction. They would begin their search at the inn where the ransom had been left, although Damian doubted they would learn much. "We'll arrive at the Horse and Hounds for afternoon tea," he said, sitting back and just enjoying looking at her. Was Luke right? Would Lady Diana be his undoing? It should have worried him more than it did, but the inappropriate image of waking to find her in his bed every morning, naked, entered his mind. He could only return her smile.

Chapter Twelve

IT WAS LATE afternoon, and they'd traveled for miles in the carriage. Diana tried to ignore the troubling emotions tugging at her. While the chance of finding Anne remained uppermost in her mind, she was very aware of being alone with Ballantine. She'd come to terms with the strength of her feelings for him, although it seemed extraordinary she felt this way when they'd met such a short time ago. And she'd come to the startling conclusion that she'd never felt such desire for any other man. It had been easy in the past to resist those who'd flirted with her, to whom, once they'd been out of her orbit, she'd never gave another thought. But Ballantine. Here was a man she respected, desired, and she could so easily love. In fact, she was half in love with him already. But she also knew if she wasn't careful, it could end in heartache.

He constantly drew her gaze, his broad shoulders and long, powerful legs in their glossy boots, carefully positioned not to touch hers.

"The afternoon has grown warm." He shrugged off his coat and sat back in his shirt and olive-green waistcoat with gold buttons. Loosening his cravat, he revealed a tuft of dark hair at the base of his olive-skinned throat.

"It is quite warm." As Diana shrugged out of her pelisse, Ballantine moved over to her seat to help her.

"Allow me." While he drew the pelisse off her shoulders, Diana breathed in clean, masculine sweat, starched linens, a fresh cologne scented with citrus, and a hint of boot polish.

"Thank you," she said primly, not wanting him to know how his proximity affected her. She was conscious of how insignificant a life she had lived compared to his.

He, however, appeared to be unaffected by their nearness. With her pelisse removed, he resumed his seat opposite her. She looked up while folding it to find his dark, thoughtful eyes upon her. What did he think about her? She hated him believing this race across the countryside to be a foolish waste of time. He swallowed, and her breath caught. How would the skin on his throat feel if she pressed her lips there? Would it be smooth or slightly prickly? Did people do *it* in carriages? The small space suddenly grew too hot. Her chest tight, she coughed.

His eyes became concerned. "My brother's carriage isn't well sprung. I shall have to take Luke to task. I hope the bumps and swaying aren't making you feel unwell."

She shook her head. Of course Ballantine wouldn't have arrived in his own coach. He wouldn't have wished to advertise his presence alone with her, for both their sakes. Who knew which people put up at this inn? Some might know either of them. They could become the subject of gossip, and then her father would hear of it. She suffered a pang of guilt. She'd never seriously considered the imposition she'd placed on Ballantine by begging him to take her.

"We shall be at the inn within the hour. A glass of wine and some supper will make you feel more the thing."

"You are too kind," she murmured.

He laughed. "Not at all. How formal you sound, Lady Diana. You're not regretting your decision to come?"

"Oh, no, absolutely not." And after supper, she and Ballantine would sleep under the same roof, unchaperoned. Anything could happen! She had little knowledge of what that might entail. Only that she would want Ballantine to instigate it.

When she'd been younger, Diana had had a crush on a groom in her father's stables. She had sashayed up to him one day and dared him to kiss her. He'd gone purple in the face and backed away. Embarrassed, she'd told Anne, but then they'd laughed about it. The poor man would have been afraid of dismissal. *Anne!* Diana gasped. Where was Anne? What must she be enduring? Had that horrid man taken advantage of her? Or worse? Killed her, as everyone else seemed to think? She couldn't bear it. Tears sprung to her eyes.

Ballantine leaned forward and seized her gloved hand. "You seem distressed."

"I am a little." Her pulse thudding, she studied how his long-fingered hand had enveloped hers in a comforting grip. She had an overwhelming urge to climb into his lap and sob against his chest. She fought to steady her voice. "I was thinking about Anne, and whether we can discover something helpful at the inn."

He released her hand, sitting back again. "Don't get your hopes up too much. After so much time has passed, the trail will probably have gone cold."

His unwelcome opinion made her more annoyed than sad. She glowered at him. "I won't accept that until there is no other option."

He gazed at her approvingly. "Well, that's more like the Lady Diana I've become familiar with. You don't give up easily, do you?"

"Not until I'm forced to." So he thought he knew her? It would take him aback should he be privy to her thoughts. Although she doubted he'd be easily shocked. Would it intrigue him to learn of her raging desire for him to become her lover? He'd probably continue to keep her at a distance. Rather like the groom in her father's stables, she thought, annoyed. Then there was that kiss. Ballantine was an earl and would not be afraid of her father, but he would be wary of becoming trapped into marriage. It wasn't flattering, but she was prepared to accept the most obvious reason. He performed vital work for the country.

Dangerous work. Had a gunshot caused the wound in his arm?

As he watched her, a smile tugged at his mouth and turned his eyes to warm chocolate. He looked more approachable and exceedingly attractive. She couldn't help responding while praying she would prove him wrong about Anne. Diana smiled back and, to distract herself, turned to gaze out the window.

The carriage proceeded along a country road where the view was unchanging for miles: trees, meadows, hedges, sheep and cows, the odd horse in a paddock, or a farmhouse in the distance. Toll roads were usually busy with travelers on foot or in vehicles, but few were about today. Heavens, but for his coachman and groom, she and Ballantine were alone. She trusted him implicitly, but what danger did he think could befall them? Gunmen had attacked his carriage before. Who were they? Her father had told her highwaymen were not common in that part of the county. Whether this was true, or he wished to reassure her, she didn't know. Ballantine had tucked a pistol beneath the seat when they'd first entered the carriage. Remembering it, her shoulders tightened.

"I'm glad you brought your pistol," she said. "I was tempted to bring Papa's dueling pistol, too, but he might have missed it."

"I'm relieved that you didn't," he said wryly. "I always travel armed. Surely, the duke would travel with guards?"

He was attempting to put her at her ease, but she knew they might have to deal with some dangerous people. "Yes. Papa never travels without his armed footmen." It had reassured her after the criminals had abducted Anne.

"Is your arm better?" she asked him.

"Yes. Thank you. Just a graze."

While annoyed he didn't trust her with the truth, she admitted spies must, by the very nature of their work, be secretive. Despite that, she had to ask. "Did you find what you sought at Holland House?"

He cocked an eyebrow. "It proved satisfactory."

"Was Lord Montgomery involved?"

"I don't know."

"The man is thoroughly dislikable. I wonder what he wished to see my father about."

"You shall find out soon enough, I daresay." Ballantine altered his position, drawing his foot from where he'd rested it on his knee, and accidentally nudged her half boot. "I beg your pardon." He tucked his legs to one side, looking uncomfortable.

"It must be difficult…being so tall…traveling in a carriage, I mean," she said, hastily shifting her gaze from his pantaloons where they clung to his thighs, and the intriguing shape above. She remembered how his mouth had felt against hers. Firm, and demanding, and utterly thrilling. Her tongue traced her lips, recalling it.

When she dared to raise her eyes to his, he drew in a breath and shifted in his seat. "I don't care for coach travel. My preference is to ride, if possible."

"You are very good to do this for me," she said in a rush. "I am deeply in your debt."

"No need. I confess to being as eager as you to discover the truth. But not so confident about the outcome. We must wait to see if anything comes from this jaunt." He folded his arms.

Doubting Thomas. But as he'd obliged her, he may say whatever he wished.

"Lady Diana," Ballantine said, his eyes searching hers. "If you wish us to continue on this quest, there are two things you must not do."

"Oh? What are they?"

"Don't prod me for information on things that don't concern you, and don't do that thing with your tongue."

Her eyes widened and scorching heat spread from her chest down over her body. "I shall try to keep it in mind." She turned back to the window to hide a grin and didn't miss his soft laugh.

"AH, HERE WE are," Damian said as the carriage turned into the forecourt of the Hare and Hounds, a two-story, whitewashed building with a small garden.

Lady Diana looked about. "It seems a harmless place with those people sitting outdoors on benches in the sun."

"Waiting for the stage coach, most likely. I hope they leave soon so I can examine that wall. A rather futile exercise, but we might learn more from the innkeeper."

Damian preferred few of his staff to be involved in this affair, hence the absence of a footman. He alighted and assisted Lady Diana, as his most trusted groom removed their luggage from the rear of the carriage. An ostler emerged from the inn to greet them and direct the carriage to the stable yard.

When Damian escorted Lady Diana inside, where savory smells emanated from the kitchen, the innkeeper, having hastily judged his guests rank, waited to attend them. He bowed his head. "Greystones, sir, madam. How can I help you?"

"Beaufort, and this is Miss Ridley. We require separate chambers for me and my cousin, if you please, Greystones," Damian said.

The innkeeper looked pained. "I have only one bedchamber available. It has a private parlor. As you can see, during this fine spring weather, the inn is full." He wrung his hands. "But of course I can move someone into a maid's room. I'm sure it won't be a problem."

"No, please don't move people about on our behalf. The bedchamber will suffice for both of us," Lady Diana said quickly.

Damian thought better of arguing with her when he noted the determined expression in her eyes. It would only make Greystones suspicious. "We shall be here for one night. I'll sleep in the parlor."

"Don't be silly, Damian. You are too tall for a sofa." She turned to the innkeeper. "Mr. Greystones, could you provide me with a truckle bed?"

Lady Diana never failed to surprise him, but Damian had to

admit he enjoyed hearing his name on her lips.

"Certainly," the innkeeper said, obviously relieved. "We will soon serve supper in the dining room. The inn has an excellent cook."

"I would like my luggage to be brought to my chamber," Lady Diana said. She turned to Damian. "I'll join you downstairs shortly, in the parlor."

With severe misgivings, Damian watched her follow the maid upstairs. "I wonder if you could help us, Greystones. We are here to make inquiries about an incident that occurred at your inn some weeks ago."

The heavy grooves on Greystones's forehead deepened. "Yes, my lord?"

"Lady Anne Daintith's kidnappers collected the ransom from here."

The innkeeper's mouth pulled down. "A tragic business. They'd hidden the money in our garden wall, of all places. I knew nothing about it until a Bow Street runner came a few days later. Then a maid mentioned having seen something stuffed in between the stones. A pity she didn't tell me about it straight away."

"I have heard the story and find it of great interest. Can you show me where?"

The innkeeper looked startled but then smiled. "Of course. I suppose people have been talking about it as far as London, haven't they? Can't say whether it's good or bad for business, though. This way, sir." He led the way out of the building and across the lawn. People chatted and laughed together, enjoying the warm day.

"They shoved it inside here." Greystones pointed to a large crevice in the rock wall.

"What an extraordinary business!" Damian squatted down and peered into the cleft. Nothing there now. If it had rained, the ransom wouldn't have been protected. It seemed an unexpected choice for the kidnappers to make. Someone must have been on hand to snatch the money away as soon as it had been left, which led him to believe it was most likely one of Greystones's staff. "Do you have any idea why they would have chosen your establishment, sir?"

Greystones shrugged his beefy shoulders. "The Bow Street runner talked to all my servants but found no answer."

"A friend at Bow Street told me of this crime. Seeing as we were passing through, I said I'd look into the matter. I should like to question them before we depart in the morning."

"Certainly, although one of my servants has since left."

"When was this?"

"Just before Bow Street called. Joseph Smythe. He was only just hired, too. Worked in the stables."

"His reason for leaving? Or was he let go?"

"No. He expressed the wish to find work closer to his mother's home."

"Do you know where he works now?" Damian asked as they returned to the inn.

"I wish I could help you, Mr. Beaufort. This has created a lot of unwelcome interest."

"Might you know where his mother lives?

"I do, as it happens," Greystones said eagerly. "Smythe's ma came to visit him the day before he left. Told a maid she lives near Chitterne, about twenty miles from here."

Damian nodded. "Thank you. You've been helpful. I'll have a brandy in the parlor while I wait for my cousin."

"Certainly, Mr. Beaufort."

Ten minutes later, Lady Diana joined Damian in the parlor. She had changed into a green-and-white striped gown. She looked endearing, her eyes shining with excitement, and he found her far too appealing.

In the dining room, the meal was plain fare but well cooked. Cauliflower soup, roast hare—the inn's specialty, rhubarb and custard, cheese and a plate of nuts. As they dined, he related his conversation with Greystones.

She put down her wineglass, her eyes wide with interest. "So this fellow, Joseph Smythe, left Greystones's employment after Anne's family had paid the ransom?"

"A few days later."

"You must admit that sounds suspicious."

"Perhaps. Tomorrow, we'll visit his mother."

She smiled. "That is good news."

He wished she wouldn't get so buoyed up. "It's not much to go on."

"But it is something," she stressed.

"Let's hope so. I intend to return you to your friend's home in Bath before nightfall tomorrow."

"I don't see why you must rush. They don't expect me." With a frown, she held up her empty wineglass. "May I have another?"

Greystones hurried to their table, bottle in hand, and filled her glass before Damian questioned the wisdom of it.

When the innkeeper stepped away, she leaned across the table, displaying a tantalizing glimpse of her breasts. "And what if we come across another, even more vital lead, which keeps us away for another night? We can hardly ignore it," she whispered.

"We'll face that problem if it arises," he said, unable to resist smiling. He was confident that the next day would bring an end to this unwise enterprise, when they ran out of people to question. He enjoyed being with her too much and would like it to continue for days. *Reckless.* He thought he'd known his limitations, but she was fascinating and irrepressible, and now he wasn't sure.

Chapter Thirteen

DIANA SETTLED NERVOUSLY onto the truckle bed and pulled the bedcovers up to her chin. Ballantine had accepted the offer from a gentleman guest for another hand of cards, even though the hour had grown late. Annoyed, she stared at the comfortable, empty bed. He might at least make use of it. She would lie awake until he arrived.

When she opened her eyes again, dawn light crept through the gaps in the curtains, and somewhere, a cockerel crowed. She'd been so tired, and after drinking more wine than she was used to, she'd fallen asleep. Blinking, she sat up, surprised at being in the big bed, the truckle bed empty.

She put her hands to her cheeks and gasped, then bent to examine her nightgown, still buttoned up to the neck. He might at least have had the decency to wake her. And where was he?

Thoroughly unsettled, she threw back the covers and put her feet to the floor, snatching up the silk dressing gown she'd fortunately crammed into her bag. Shrugging into it, she tied the belt and went to the door of the private parlor. She placed her ear against the wooden panel. A soft snore came from within.

Diana pushed up the latch and opened the door a crack, wide enough to see Ballantine, his tousled, dark head resting on a pillow. She slipped inside and moved closer. Partly covered by a blanket, he stretched out the length of the sofa, his legs, with a dusting of dark hair, and his big feet protruding from the end. One bare, muscular arm rested above the blanket. Her eyes widened. Was he naked beneath it?

What had he seen when he'd moved her over to the bed? She pushed that thought hurriedly away. He'd been gentle, as she hadn't wakened. The wine must have affected her. She remembered how she'd missed her footing on the stairs when Ballantine had escorted her up to bed and how she'd had to rely on him to steady her. And *he* had ordered a second bottle of wine at dinner!

She glowered at him, sleeping so peacefully, while longing to poke him awake. Then he moved, and the blanket fell away to his waist. She stood, captivated by his wonderful physique. His skin looked so smooth, she wanted to touch him, to sweep her hands over the hollows and valleys of his sculptured chest. To touch the dark "V" of hair arrowing down... With a gasp, her gaze flew to his lean face, his level, dark brows, the sensual curve of his mouth. And she wanted so much more. He defined masculine in a way she'd never thought of. She could imagine him staring down a villain with a sword in his hand or a gun. He would be lethal.

She fought to control her rapid breathing. What if she startled him and he woke and caught her staring at him? Like some crazed woman desperate for his body? She turned away as she tried not to giggle.

"I trust I didn't disturb you last night," came the husky voice from the sofa.

"Oh!" She spun around. "You had no need to move me into the bed. I was perfectly comfortable."

"Were you?" He propped his head up on his elbow and gazed complacently at her. "I thought it better to change the sleeping arrangements, for propriety's sake."

She pressed a hand against her forehead, aware of a nasty throbbing. The wine. "I hope you had a horrible night."

"That's not very kind of you. Slept like a baby." He took hold of the blanket. "Unless you wish to see more of me in my natural state, I advise you to turn away."

Diana whirled around. "I do not," she lied, listening to the rustling behind her.

His hands rested on her shoulders as he turned her around. He had pulled on his pantaloons, but the sight of him was still overwhelming. "I do not intend to take liberties with your reputation, Lady Diana. *If* I can help it."

Or risk being forced to marry me, she thought. He didn't want her. Perhaps didn't desire her enough to… "I appreciate your …"

Before she could complete the sentence, his mouth was on hers. His hands molded around her waist, then moved down to cup her bottom and pull her closer so that her breasts pressed against his bare chest through the thin silk, and lower down… Was that…? She breathed in his musky scent as his lips explored hers and clutched his bare shoulder, satiny beneath her fingers. His beard rasped against her cheek. Murmuring his name against his lips, her hands boldly strayed over his back, feeling the powerful muscles at play.

Then he broke the kiss, apparently far less willing to continue than she, and turned away to pick up his shirt from the chair.

Diana felt unsure of her footing. She dragged in a breath and stared at him.

"That's not to say I don't want to continue this to its ultimate conclusion," he said in a gruff voice. "Men have a lower boiling point. So stop tempting me. Return to your chamber and dress. Ask the maid to bring me coffee and hot water. I shall see you at breakfast. And after I speak to the staff, we will leave."

She glared at him, struggling with outrage, although he had a point. A flush rose to her face. "I'll be ready." She left the parlor.

Now very embarrassed, she directed the maid to take Ballantine's coffee into the parlor next door, while she drank her tea and faced the truth. She had wanted Ballantine for her lover and had seized the opportunity to share the bedchamber with him. Intent on keeping her safe, he'd resisted, remaining firm in his intention to return her to Bath before nightfall, untouched. She sagged in the chair. How could he understand what lay behind this hunger that drove her? If not love, then affection, companionship, and intimacy with a man she liked and desired? A man of her choice, not her father's. How would she face him after this? Would it be better to admit this trip had been unwise from the outset and return to Bath? *No.* She must not lose sight of why she'd come. They were close to finding Anne. She could feel it.

Diana finished her tea and went to take down her spare primrose muslin from the peg where she'd hung it. Putting it on a chair, she poured hot water the maid had brought into the basin and washed. How wonderful it was to have his arms around her, his mouth on hers, and his large, warm body pressing against hers. She had wanted to lie down with him. To feel the weight of him lying over her. While her longing for him to touch her shocked her, this was how she had always imagined it should be between a man and a woman. They seemed to fit so perfectly together. Or would if they became lovers. Her breath hitched. Would she find such bliss with someone else? Certainly none of those she'd met in the past, or the gentlemen her father had introduced to her. *Papa!* She'd given little thought to home since she'd left. On her return, would she have to deal with yet another suitor? Might it be Montgomery? Surely, he hadn't come to persuade her father to agree to their marriage? The thought made her stomach roil, and she quickly dismissed it as nonsense. Her father had turned him down once; surely, he would again.

But Papa was determined to see her married, and soon. He firmly believed she'd be happier with her own establishment and bemoaned the absence of her mother to advise her. Knowing he grew tired of her evasions, she rubbed the goose flesh on her arms. Not old, and still attractive to women, it was possible Papa could remarry and have more children, and she would be demoted to secondary importance in the house in which she'd grown up. A spinster, helping to raise them while clashing with her new stepmother. Even with that last dreadful thought, marrying Lord Montgomery or someone like him appalled her.

IN THE BREAKFAST room, most of the tables were occupied, and the warm aromas of coffee, eggs, bacon, and toast filled the air. Damian and Lady Diana took a seat by the window, the sky beyond it an arch of blue with nary a cloud. No sign of rain, thankfully, as they had many miles to cover if he wanted to have her back in Bath by the end of the day.

She fussed with her serviette, avoiding his gaze. He doubted that would last long. Lady Diana was not one to remain submissive and silent. When he'd entered the bedchamber last night and found her asleep in the truckle bed, with the blanket sliding off onto the floor, he saw how uncomfortable she was. She slept deeply after consuming three glasses of wine with dinner. More than she was used to, he'd hazard a guess. He had fought his desire to get close, to enjoy every delightful inch of her should she waken and hold out her arms to him. What sort of man would he be to take advantage of an inebriated woman? And lord, what a mess it would cause. As he didn't trust himself, he would sleep in the parlor. Lady Diana only needed to look at him in a certain way to send blood sizzling through his veins, and if she gave him any encouragement, it would be too hard to resist her. But he couldn't leave her like this. The night was cool, and she might become chilled.

Fortunately, she hadn't stirred when he'd pulled off the covers and scooped her up, or he would have been in for an argument. One he might have lost. How enticing she had been, so soft and warm in his arms as he'd held her against his chest, still deeply asleep, her thick, golden-brown plait dangling down. The flowery scent of her hair, and her soft, unfettered breasts he longed to touch, to kiss, had bewitched him. But in repose, he had to admit she'd looked positively angelic.

He suspected Lady Diana didn't fully understand the consequences of them flaunting society's rules. With a regretful sigh, he'd laid her on the bed. Her nightgown had ridden up, and for a moment, he'd stood transfixed by her milky-skinned, smooth thighs barely hiding her sex, then, murmuring, "Satan get behind me," and considering himself all kinds of a fool, he'd pulled her nightgown down over her long, slim legs.

Nestling her pert bottom into the mattress, she had uttered a soft snore.

Grinning, Damian had covered her with the blanket, grabbed his luggage, the pillow and quilt from the truckle bed, and left the room before he could find an excuse to remain.

"I was wrong. Ballantine," Lady Diana said, her blue eyes troubled over the rim of her teacup. "I realize it now."

"Wrong? How?" He disliked seeing her upset, and even more that he might have been the cause of it.

She shrugged her slim shoulders in the dainty, yellow gown. "I should not have placed you in such a position. I've made you uncomfortable."

His mouth quirked up. "Not in the way you might think. This attraction goes both ways. But one of us has to keep their head. And as I am older, it must be me."

She raised her chin, her eyes widening at his confession. *Hell.* It was hardly a secret. He could barely keep his hands off her. It was a joy just to look at her. *Dash it all.* The pleasing vision of her at his breakfast table every morning swept unwelcome into his mind. But he would not be there, he reminded himself. He'd be off on some mission, and she would be alone.

"Coming on this journey, I meant," she said, flushing.

"I am not one to bow to pressure." He picked up his coffee cup. "If I hadn't wanted to come, I would have refused."

"Why did you, then?"

"Why? I thought your cause was a valid one." He admitted to himself there was more to it that he had avoided examining too closely. But it was doubtful they'd discover anything of importance in one day. Although someone should look into it. "I could have a Bow Street Runner continue the search?"

"That's wasting precious time." She frowned. "Bow Street already looked, and they gave up too easily. You don't believe we'll find Anne, either."

"There's always that chance." He smiled. "Perhaps we can discuss this further once we are in the carriage," he said, aware that they shouldn't delve too deep into their feelings. Another warning note sounded loudly in his mind. He took little heed of it. "It has troubled me to see you so worried about your friend."

"You are kind," she said, reaching for the jam.

Kind was not a word he'd apply to himself. But it would do. Impatient to be on the road again, he sawed his bacon.

Mr. Barrow, the gentleman with whom Damian had played cards the previous evening, stopped by their table with a cheery smile, apparently undeterred by Damian soundly beating him. His main purpose of befriending the fellow had been to have it put about that he'd slept on the sofa in their private parlor, as his cousin, Miss Ridley, the name Lady Diana had chosen for herself, had taken the last bedchamber to be had.

Barrow, a portly fellow with an important air, introduced himself to Miss Ridley and commiserated with Damian in his loud baritone about him having to doss down on a sofa. "And you, such a large gentleman."

"My cousin is extremely gallant," Lady Diana said with a smile. "He hasn't complained, although I suspect he has a crick in his neck this morning."

Barrow chuckled and, with a slight bow, went to join his party.

Damian drank the last of his coffee, put down the cup, and pushed back his chair. "I'll pay the bill and see to the bags. When you are ready, wait in the vestibule. I'll question the kitchen staff."

"I'll come with you."

"No sense in that," he said. "I'll have more success on my own."

"Well, with the cook and the maids, no doubt," she said with a huff. "What about the rest of the staff?"

"I spoke to the others, earlier, with little result."

"Oh, that is disappointing. But we do have a something we can follow up on today. Who knows where that will take us?"

"Back to Bath by the end of the day," Damian said, causing her to glower at him.

Lady Diana was akin to handling a hot coal.

In the kitchen with the oven fire blazing, the cook, a plump, cheery woman, and the kitchen maids scuttling around, had little to impart. A freckled-faced stableboy munching on toast slathered with honey, said, "That Joe Smythe, who worked in the stables, was shifty-eyed."

The cook hushed him. "The gentleman ain't interested in the likes of you, Harry," she said. "And wipe up that dripping honey, before someone measures their length!"

Harry hastily swallowed the last of his toast and rushed to obey.

"No need to shush him," Damian said mildly. "Why do you think that, Harry?"

"Had a visitor come to the inn," he said, down on his knees, scrubbing the floor. "I seen them out the back of the stables with their heads together."

"Did you hear what they said?"

He shook his ginger head. "No, but Joe took off a few days later."

Damian thanked Cook for the half-dozen buttered raisin scones she'd given him for the journey and went in search of Lady Diana. Wearing her bonnet and pelisse, she waited for him on the porch.

"While I was waiting for you, I questioned the maid, Sally, about Smythe," she said, hurrying toward him. "Apparently, they shared more than a friendship in the short time he was here. She was angry because he left without saying goodbye to her, so she had no compunction in telling me all about him. Apparently, he'd admitted he used to work for a Lord Daintith, while under another name."

"Well done!" Damian grinned at her. "It appears this Joe is the fellow we are looking for."

"I find it very encouraging, don't you?" she said, looking pleased.

"I do. We might learn more about him from his mother."

"I feel sure we are on the right track." Lady Diana eyed his parcel. "What have you there?"

He smiled. "Raisin scones. Cook thought we might get peckish on our journey."

She took the parcel from him with a wry expression. "No doubt you charmed her. But how thoughtful of her! If you purchase a bottle of wine from Greystones, we can stop for luncheon." She grimaced and put a hand to her forehead. "On second thought, perhaps not wine."

Damian smiled sympathetically. "Ah, here's the carriage," he said as it rattled around the corner from the stable yard.

Shortly afterward, it bowled along the road toward the Smythes' cottage, and Damian added what the stableboy had said about the man who'd come to see Joe. She sat back and nodded thoughtfully.

"It doesn't fill in the gaps," he added. "Something doesn't add up."

"I think it does," she said earnestly. "He must have sought employment here after he left Anne's father's stables. And then he disappeared again. It is clear they were planning something. I can't help feeling we are getting closer to finding out where Anne is." She frowned, as if daring him to refute it.

He merely nodded and leaned back against the squab, studying her lovely face beneath the brim of the flowery bonnet, a blue bow tied at the side of her chin. He would hate to witness her bitter disappointment when this search proved unsuccessful.

Chapter Fourteen

A s the sun climbed higher in the sky, Diana and Lord Ballantine were still several miles from their destination. When the carriage approached an inn, Ballantine ordered the coachman to pull into the forecourt.

"Are we to have luncheon here?" Diana asked.

"No. I think we've taken enough chances. Stay in the carriage. I'll fetch us something to eat." He winked. "Cooks always like me." Before leaving the carriage, he turned to her and smiled. "Shall we have a picnic?"

"Oh, yes." She imagined cooks would like him. And not just because he was handsome. While he went by the name of Beaufort, it was clear he was a wealthy nobleman. She watched his fluid stride as he walked toward the inn. Ballantine was full of surprises. How would she settle down to her humdrum life after this?

When he emerged ten minutes later, he carried a package and a wicker basket. He handed the package to the groom and entered the carriage, bringing with him the delicious smell of roasted chicken.

"What have you there?" Diana asked, unable to stem her curiosity. She was suddenly ravenous, having eaten only a piece of toast and jam at breakfast. She would bring the raisin scones for dessert.

"Why didn't you eat more at breakfast?" he asked.

Diana grinned. "I was nervous."

"Why?"

"I was nervous about Anne. And it crossed my mind I might meet someone I knew."

"But you were still willing to take that chance?"

She widened her eyes. "Of course."

He chuckled as the carriage took off down the road.

A few miles on, Ballantine ordered the carriage to stop when they came to a green meadow dotted with wildflowers. He grabbed a rug from beneath the seat and left the carriage carrying the basket. Handing it to the groom, he helped Diana descend.

They left the driver and groom to enjoy their own feast, with bottles of ale, seated near the horses.

Carrying the basket, Ballantine firmly clasped Diana's hand, and they strolled deeper into the meadow toward a copse of trees. The sound of a tinkling brook reached them.

"A musical accompaniment," she said, laughing. "How did you manage it?"

He grinned. "I always plan ahead."

Beneath the leafy boughs of a chestnut, he spread the rug on a level patch of dense grass and helped her to sit. She took off her bonnet, loving the feeling of the sun on her face, although it would have appalled her grandmother, and then removed her gloves. Nearby, the small brook rushed over pebbles so clear, you could see the bottom. A bird in the tree above called to the flock to come in hope of crumbs.

Kneeling beside the basket, Ballantine removed plates, glasses, and serviettes, the roasted chicken, bread and butter, and a bottle of lemonade.

They sat and ate companionably. The delicious meat was cooked to perfection. When Diana had a piece of the breast, she couldn't resist licking her fingers.

Ballantine paused while pouring the lemonade. He raised an eyebrow.

Diana fought not to giggle and snatched up a serviette to finish wiping her hands. It hadn't been intentional, but she delighted in being able to stir him in this way, which was new to her. Conscious of them being alone, she took the glass from him and sipped the refreshingly cool and tart drink. "How far have we to go?" she asked, nibbling a buttered scone while wanting to break the silence that had grown between them. Nerves tightened her chest, and Ballantine seemed suddenly like a coiled spring. Were they closer to finding Anne?

"About eight miles." He drew up a leg in those tight pantaloons and clasped his knee with his hands, his thoughtful gaze on her.

She recalled how he looked half-naked and hastily tamped down the strong desire to reach out and touch him. What would he do if she did? She brushed crumbs from her skirts. "I hope you don't feel this is a waste of your time."

"No. Whatever the outcome."

She wanted to ask him to elaborate but held her tongue. It was as if their conversation had nothing to do with what hovered unspoken between them. Their kiss was still uppermost in her thoughts, and perhaps in his. She wanted more. More of his kisses, his muscular body, his smell, his taste. She wanted to sleep with him beside her, resting her head on his chest. To wake in the morning and share the days with him. Seek his opinion about some ideas she'd had to make her life fulfilling. It couldn't be just motherhood, although she would welcome children. There had to be something more.

"We should pack up and get on our way," she said, aware of his gaze on her, her strained voice sounding odd to her.

Ignoring her need for a little reassurance, she packed the hamper. Although she wanted more from him, she would never ask it, not after he'd virtually accused her of inviting him to seduce her. Thinking of it still stung. A lady should have been demure. Hadn't her governess drummed that into her? Anne would have agreed. She was effortlessly always a picture of decorum.

"Rest awhile." He tucked his hands behind his head and crossed his booted feet.

"Don't you plan to return to Bath before nightfall?" Even though Bath was not far, if one judged it as the crow flew, it seemed doubtful they'd reach there today. She could hardly arrive at Penny's after dark. They might be forced to spend another night at an inn. Or was that just a wonderful dream?

"What is it you want from life, Diana?"

About to add a plate to the basket, she looked up at him, surprised by his informal use of her name, which was understandable in the circumstances, but also his softer tone, which sounded more intimate. He invited confidences she didn't feel comfortable revealing. He might find them trivial or foolish. Women had far fewer options than men. His gaze rested on her mouth, and her heart began that incessant hammering. "To be useful, and content, I suppose," she said, fighting to keep her voice level. "Doesn't everyone? To spend my life with a man who understands me. To share my dreams with the man I love." It was a dream, not the reality. She must do as her father wished. But she still wanted to experience everything she dreamed of with Ballantine before they parted. Would life then become more bearable? She couldn't convince herself that she could live happily with her memories. She wanted so much more.

"Love?" He sounded almost harsh. "That's a hard emotion to define."

Then he hasn't been in love. "Until one finds the right person."

"You've never fallen even a little in love?"

Yes, she thought, *with you.* But she shook her head. "Papa is determined to see me married before the year ends. He chooses my prospective husbands, and so far, I haven't even liked them."

"What was wrong with them?"

"They were perfectly respectable, I suppose. Perhaps I want too much."

Diana waited for him to disagree. He didn't. *Lud, he was an annoying man.* "Why are you so determined not to marry?" she asked, determined to make this conversation more about him.

"My work prevents it. I am often out of the country."

"So are many in the government or in business. They still marry and have children."

"That arrangement doesn't suit everyone."

No, not a passionate man like Ballantine. A man who fed on excitement. Not to mention this work he did for the crown, which was vital to the country and must have been very dangerous. She would be a good wife for him because she would let him go off without complaint. She didn't believe marriage would give her the right to make unreasonable demands. But would he be unfaithful? That was one thing she couldn't accept after seeing how much it had hurt her mother. She'd even travel with him. Women followed the drum, after all. But not spies, she supposed. Their lives would be very different. Surely, even spies wished for hearth and home when they returned to England?

She kept these thoughts to herself while she packed the remaining crockery in the hamper. Once she'd closed the lid, he stood and gathered up the blanket, tucking it under his arm. She offered her his hand. He pulled her to her feet with her hat in her hand and their gazes locked. Her heart began that annoying hammering again. The breeze strengthened, stirring the leaves overhead and playing havoc with her hair before she could don her hat, unraveling a lock and sending it flying across her face. She *tsked* and put her hand up to order it.

"Allow me. Stand still." He dropped the blanket and tucked the errant lock behind her ear. Then stood regarding it. "You have pretty hair."

"It's just brown. Blondes were more in demand during the Season." *And those with large bosoms,* she imagined, recalling her father's paintings.

"The sunlight brings out the gold in your hair." He put his hands on her shoulders to steady her on the uneven grass. "Wait, there's another curl about to escape the pins."

Terribly pleased he liked her hair, she couldn't help wondering how experienced he was with women's tresses. As he angled the pin back into what she feared was like an untidy owl's nest, she availed herself of the opportunity to study him at close quarters, his sharp cheekbones, his smooth skin, and his long, black eyelashes. He stood so close that his breath, scented with lemons and raisins, warmed her cheek. She began leaning toward him.

"It shan't blow in your eyes now," he said hoarsely.

Without thinking, she traced her finger over his smooth jaw. He'd shaved this morning. His troubled, brown eyes locked with her own gaze, and after a strained moment, he took her hand and kissed the palm. "Shall we go?"

The touch of his lips on her skin lingered after he drew away and picked up the rug and the basket.

Why had she done that? The need to touch him, to be close, perplexed her as she pulled on her gloves, donned her bonnet and tied the ribbons.

He offered her his free hand to help her over the rough meadow grass, and they made their way silently back to the carriage.

She welcomed the clasp of his long fingers. Even if he didn't love her, he cared about her. It warmed her through to her core. As if she had gained a chivalrous knight who would slay dragons for her. To be fair, Papa had done his best to raise her after her mother had died, but he had his art, and as a parent, must release her into another man's hands. She'd never felt so protected. Not since her mother had wrapped her up in her love. *Don't get used to it! This will all end within a few hours.* Endeavoring to keep up with Ballantine's long stride, she wished things were different. But what good did wishing ever do?

Diana pushed these thoughts away, already keen to go on. Within a few hours, they might learn the truth, but she went cold with fear at what that might be.

DAMIAN'S STUBBORN BRAIN kept telling him Diana was his. That no other woman could come close to the way he felt about her. But it didn't matter, even if she felt the same. And he suspected she might. She liked to tease him, to touch him. Resisting her almost drove him mad. Remembering the way she'd responded to his kiss, pressing herself against him, her soft hands moving over his back. He hadn't suffered this level of frustration without acting on it since a callow youth. His body ached with wanting her. Even touching her, threading his fingers through hers as they walked back to the carriage, made him want her. Want much more time with her. To discover everything about her: her funny quirks and endearing foibles.

He sensed himself edging recklessly closer to something he couldn't control. Odd, when he'd faced far worse trouble with the confidence he'd always handle it. But this intense feeling, as if, once they parted, he'd go back to a life he now recognized as empty, despite all the successes he'd had on his missions, left him oddly defenseless. Within days, he could leave England and must keep reminding himself of the fact. Undertaking dangerous work for Scovell needed his full attention. With Diana on his mind, he could slip up and endanger himself, and perhaps others. He tightened his jaw. Once they were comfortably seated and the carriage had gotten underway, he took control, as he probably should have done days ago. "We must return to Bath after visiting the Smythes' cottage. I intend to leave you at the Howards' home before day's end. Then return to London."

Diana's dark-blue eyes met his. "Yes, I understand, Ballantine."

The determination to pursue this quest to the bitter end had faded from her eyes. Had she come to believe as he did, they would not find Lady Anne alive? It was his fault if so, and he was sorry for it. He'd humored Diana on this quest, while remaining skeptical, but he wanted to find the answer to this mystery as much as she did.

Chapter Fifteen

DIANA FOUGHT BITTER disappointment at Ballantine's emphatic statement. He didn't want to risk spending another night with her, and she had too much pride to show that he'd hurt her. In spite of knowing he had never been hers nor ever would be. But must she soon have to give up her search for Anne, too? Not wishing him to read her thoughts, she sat forward on the seat and stared out the window, searching for a sign of the cottage.

After traveling several miles, a building appeared on a narrow strip of fenced land. Diana's chest tightened, and she turned back to Ballantine. "Do you think that's the Smythes' house?"

"Might be." Ballantine ordered the coachman to stop.

A weedy path led up to a shabby cottage where white paint peeled from the window frames and the front door. "It looks deserted," she said, turning to him.

"Shall we find out?"

Opening the carriage door, Ballantine leaped to the ground. With his hands warm and strong at her waist, he swung her down. They made their way along a muddy path that led to the front door. Her heart sank. Surely, the villain could not keep Anne a prisoner here? As Ballantine knocked, she swallowed, her mouth suddenly dry.

Diana gripped her hands together. She appreciated Ballantine's calm touch on her back as they waited.

Footfalls shuffled closer to the door. It opened a crack and a lady with graying brown hair peered out. She looked them up and down, her eyes widening.

"Mrs. Smythe?" Ballantine ventured.

Dressed in a faded gown of indeterminate color, the woman opened the door a fraction wider. "What do ye want?"

"We need to speak to your son, Joseph, madam."

Her cloudy, hazel eyes narrowed. "What do ye want with Joe?"

"Does he live here?"

"He's not here now."

"Where is he, Mrs. Smythe? It is very important that we speak to him," Diana said, finding her voice. "He may be able to help us."

The woman's hazel eyes looked widened. "I told 'em no good would come of it."

Ballantine leaned closer. "Come of what? Mrs. Smythe?"

She shuffled backward. "I won't say no more. You'll have to speak to 'em."

"Who are they?"

"I had nothing to do with it."

"Then if you'll kindly give us his direction, we shall leave you in peace."

"Joe works at the farm down the road apace."

She began to close the door, but Ballantine put up his hand to hold it open. "How far is it?"

"Five miles. Just past the woods. Tell Joe I warned 'im this would not go well for him." She huffed. "But he thinks he's smarter than his ma."

Ballantine let go of the door, and it slammed shut.

Diana was grateful for Ballantine's support as they retreated down the path. Her legs shook and her heart galloped. Were they close to the truth? Close to finding out what had happened to Anne?

She barely noticed the view beyond the carriage window: cows in the green meadows, fields planted with spring crops and some lying fallow. They entered the small woodland and then emerged into sunlight.

Half a mile down the road, a gate in a stone wall stood open. On a rise above the trees, they could see the roof of a building.

Diana swallowed, fighting to remain calm. "That must be the farmhouse Smythe's mother spoke of, where Joe works." She searched Ballantine's uneasy eyes.

He nodded. "Let's find out."

They left the carriage on the road and walked through the gate and along a gravel drive through the well-kept grounds, the bushes pruned, the garden beds in full flower perfuming the air in the warm sun. *A woman's touch*, Diana thought. Well-tended farmland stretched out on either side, and to the rear was a large barn and some sheds. Would Joe speak to them? Tell them the truth? If it proved a dead end, Ballantine would take her back to Bath. She wasn't sure she could bear it.

They rounded the copse of trees, and a farmhouse came into view: a long, brick, two-story dwelling with a wide verandah along the front, smoke rising into the sky from a chimney in the slate roof.

Would these people know anything about the kidnapping? It seemed unlikely. Her knees threatened to buckle, and she clung desperately to Ballantine's arm.

He ushered her up onto the verandah, where there was a rocking chair with a basket of wool and knitting needles beside it. Someone's comfortable home.

Ballantine rapped on the door.

Somewhere inside, a dog barked sharply. A maid in an apron and mobcap opened the door, and a slight, gray dog slipped out and danced around Diana's skirts.

"Toby?" Diana croaked. Surely, she must be mistaken. She bent down to pat the whippet's smooth head. Anne's dog had disappeared the same day as she had.

Ballantine crouched down to scratch the dog behind the ear, delighting the animal.

Forgetting all about Joe, Diana straightened, her throat suddenly dry. "We have come to inquire about a friend of mine. Lady Anne Daintith. Would your mistress or master know of her?"

The ginger-haired maid stared at her. "You must mean Mrs. Trent."

"Who is it, Mary?" came a voice from deep in the shadowy hallway.

Diana pushed past the maid and stumbled forward along the hall toward a woman who had just stepped into view. "Anne?" Her chest heaved and tears spilled down her cheeks.

Anne walked toward her in stately fashion, shock registering in her eyes, her belly large beneath her apron, her blonde hair in a bun beneath a small, lace cap. She sighed as she put her arms around Diana and drew her close. "I knew you'd find me someday."

"You planned this?" Diana moved back, suffering from joy, confusion, and betrayal. "You let me think you'd been..." She could not say the words for the life of her.

Anne gazed at Ballantine. "Who is this?"

"Anne, I'd like you to meet Damian Beaufort, Earl of Ballantine, who has helped me to find you." She turned to Ballantine, and saw the concern in his eyes. "Lord Ballantine, may I present Lady Anne Daintith. Or... I suppose, Lady Anne Trent?"

"I go by the name of Mrs. Trent here." Anne smiled politely. "How do you do, Lord Ballantine?" She turned back to Diana. "How did you find out where I was?" she asked, her eyes fearful. "My father hasn't found out?"

"No, Anne. We followed Joseph Smythe's trail. Your father knows nothing," Diana said. "And he won't, Anne. If you don't wish it."

Anne's shoulders drooped, but she looked relieved. "Please, come into the parlor." She turned to the maid. "Mary, bring the tea tray. We'll have the iced carrot cake."

The nicely furnished parlor, like the rest of the property, was as neat as a pin. The warm room smelled of smoke, lavender, and beeswax, which mingled with the sweet aromas of baked goods wafting from the kitchen. "I owe you an explanation, Diana. Please, will you both sit down?"

The dog settled into his basket, his tail wagging.

Fearing she might be dreaming, Diana sank onto the sofa covered in chintz while Ballantine, who had said nothing beyond the pleasantries, took an upholstered chair by the fireplace.

"My husband, Gerald Trent, worked on my father's estate at one time," Anne began.

"He told the kidnapper where to find you," Diana said, disliking him even before she met him. "Your routine after you went shopping. The route you took."

Anne shook her head.

Realization dawned inside Diana's mind. "He *was* the kidnapper. You were never in danger."

Anne chewed her lip but nodded. "Joe helped us. He and Gerald were friends, so he knew… But it was a mutual decision, Diana. Gerald and I love each other. I couldn't tell my father I was with child. Papa had arranged a marriage to a man I detested. My life would have been hellish after he discovered the child wasn't his." Her face softened, and she looked toward the door. "And I wanted to marry the man I love." Anne's smile became strained. "You think I wouldn't wish to be a farmer's wife? Being a lord's wife was not for me, and certainly not married to the haughty viscount. I am exactly where I want to be," she said, her eyes smiling as Mary brought in the tea things. "And I'm blissfully happy."

A tall, brown-haired man wearing leather breeches and a patched jacket came into the parlor in his socks. The dog left its basket and ran to greet him. He patted the dog's neck, looking surprised and wary. "I wasn't aware we had visitors." His blue eyes sought Anne's, and he received a nod of reassurance.

"Forgive me," he said. "My boots were muddy, and it's more than my life is worth to wear them in the house. If you'll excuse me, I'll change."

Anne rose and joined him at the door, taking his hand in hers. "Don't go yet, my love. I'd like you to meet my wonderful friend, Lady Diana Stafford, whom I have told you so much about. Diana will never betray us. I know she has a big heart."

Diana introduced Ballantine, who had climbed to his feet. "This has turned out far better than we feared it would, sir," Ballantine said, offering his hand.

"I am relieved to hear you say so, milord," Trent said, shaking it. "But we should not like this to become known. Please do be seated." Still uneasy, he touched Anne's arm and, with a loving smile, left the room, the dog following.

Anne poured the tea Mary had brought in while the maid served the cake, still warm from the oven.

While not what Diana would call handsome, Anne's husband had a gentle face. He obviously loved Anne. She was overwhelmed to find Anne safe but had to fight a sense of betrayal. Why hadn't Anne thought she could confide in her? She had caused so many to suffer. Soon after Anne had been taken, her mother had passed away. Did Anne know of her death? Diana hated to be the one to tell her. Her mother had expected, as Diana had, that Anne had been the perfect, demure lady who would marry for duty.

Mr. Trent returned to the room, having changed his clothes, and Ballantine immediately drew him into a conversation about farming practices. Ballantine confessed to relying on his brother to run his estate and a desire to further his knowledge for the time when he took over the reins again.

It gave Diana a glimpse into Ballantine's life. One day, he must give up his dangerous life. But when would that be?

Mr. Trent invited him to look over the farm. After their tea, the men went outside, the dog following in their wake.

"Anne. I have bad news." Diana took Anne's hand in hers as

they sat together on the sofa. "Your mother has passed away. Did you know?"

Anne nodded sadly. "Joe found out. Mama discovered she was seriously ill before I left. She knew of our plans after Gerald inherited this farm from an uncle. Knowing she would not live long, she supported us and promised to keep my secret."

Diana stared at her. "Didn't she want a fine marriage for you? One that your birthright guarantees?"

"She wanted me to be happy and knew I wouldn't be with Lord Withnell. If Papa knew of the pregnancy, I would hold no sway in whatever he decided. He would not have let me keep my baby."

"I can hardly believe it." Diana still trembled and had to put down her cup. "To find you here, happy and well, when I dreaded…" Overwhelmed, she put her hands to her face and sobbed.

"I'm so sorry, dearest." Anne moved over to hug her. "If I had told you, it would have been an even worse burden for you to carry. To attend the memorial service and have to continue to lie to my father. I couldn't ask you to do that. You will keep my secret, I know. But can I trust Lord Ballantine?"

Diana smiled through her tears as she fumbled for her handkerchief. "He is extremely good at keeping secrets. After all, we came here unescorted. Papa believes I am staying with Penny in Bath."

Anne's eyes widened, then she giggled, making Diana think sadly of times past. "I thought there was something between you two. It is unmistakable."

"What is?"

"Why, the way he looks at you. He is smitten."

Her heart squeezed, but she hurriedly discounted it. "Ballantine does not wish to marry until his hair turns gray."

Anne took hold of Diana's hand. "Ah, then it is up to you to change his mind. If anyone can do it, you can. When you wanted something, you never gave up until it was yours."

Diana gave a watery giggle. "That doesn't apply so easily to people. And especially not Ballantine."

She had always thought of Anne as one who would never flaunt society's rules. She could not have been more wrong. Perhaps it was love alone that had made Anne change her convictions. Could love change Ballantine's? Diana must not allow herself to think it. "Why not just run away?" she asked. "Why take such a chance and demand a ransom?"

Anne frowned. "Gerald did not want the ransom, but I insisted. The money was a legacy from an aunt and was to be my dowry. Papa always said the handsome dowry would ensure a man of some distinction would wish to marry me. As if I had nothing else to offer."

Diana sighed. "Am I likely to see you again?"

Tears filled Anne's eyes. She shook her head. "Letters could be dangerous."

"But I shan't find out about your baby."

"If it's a girl, I shall call her Diana."

Diana leaned her head against her friend's. "I hope the birth goes well." Relief, shock and confusion dragged her down like a weight had settled on her chest. She had lost her before, and now was to lose her again.

WHEN THEY SAID their goodbyes and settled in the carriage, Damian took one look at Diana's tender and tremulous mouth and tear-streaked face and wanted to cradle her close, to tell her she wasn't alone. It twisted his guts that he couldn't. Allowing himself some latitude, he moved to sit beside her and placed an arm around her trembling shoulders, feeling the warmth of her body through her clothes. She was tired and emotionally wrought. "I like Lady Anne's husband. He is a good man."

He pulled a handkerchief from his pocket and handed it to

her.

"Yes, I thought so." She dabbed her eyes. "But why didn't she trust me to keep her secret? She must have known I would stand by her." She blew her nose. "I thought I knew her. I was the one who never followed rules, while Anne was the obedient one."

"We don't always know what people feel deep down in their hearts."

She swiveled to gaze up at him. "Especially when they keep their secrets close."

"I'm afraid so," he admitted sadly.

"I feel as if I'm losing two friends today."

Her words stabbed at him. "You need to rest. When you arrive at the Howards', you'll feel better."

"I won't." She sighed and rested her head against his chest. "Seduce me, Damian."

He had thought of little else since he'd first met her. He wanted her. Every time he looked at her. But despite her daring and fiery nature, she was an innocent. She didn't know much about life despite her courage and determination. And she trusted him. He eased away, placing her at a safe distance, torn between burgeoning desire and the necessity to refuse her. His next mission was into the heart of France and his chance of returning alive an uncertainty. "That would not be sensible."

She removed her bonnet and put a hand to her hair. "Not everything in life must be sensible. I promise when I leave you in Bath, I will never try to see you again."

"Diana…I couldn't leave you after that."

She peeled off her gloves. "Yes, you could. The demands made on you by the crown will soon fill your life."

"If only it were that simple."

She smiled slightly. "Why is it not?" Her searching gaze held his as she unbuttoned her pelisse and slipped it from her shoulders. She ran her fingers over the bodice, drawing his eye to her breasts. Damian raised his eyebrows. Did she intend to seduce him? Her striped, modest muslin carriage gown was deceiving. It clung to the slender curves beneath.

The carriage seemed to fill with her warm scent. If he weren't so roused, her attempt at seduction would have amused him. "You believe that we could just shake hands and part afterward?"

She frowned, refusing to laugh. "Not like that, precisely. But I believe in the commitment to your country you've made. It matters more than anything else in your life at this moment. Am I not right?"

She might have been once, though not now. But considering it unwise to reveal his feelings on the matter, he shook his head.

"You don't want marriage, but you desire me, Damian."

"Are you sure this isn't just a reaction to finding Lady Anne?"

She shook her head. "Being here with you is something I'll treasure. Especially when I return home, and my father presents me with the man with whom I am to spend the rest of my life. And Papa will choose a husband who can keep his unruly daughter in control." She flushed as if she feared she was disloyal. "Not because Papa doesn't love me. But because he thinks he knows what is best for me."

Damian liked women and took care to discover their needs during an affair. He'd never left a lover feeling animosity toward him, and he didn't want this to end badly, for both their sakes. But he could not oblige her. He moved the pelisse onto the opposite seat and joined her, catching her hand in his, the touch of her soft skin, enough to fire his imagination and send his blood racing. "And when your husband discovers you are not a virgin?"

She shrugged. "What does that matter?"

"The man may be angry. Your whole life will begin with a lie."

"As I'm sure many do."

But not you, he thought. She was the most truthful woman he had ever known.

At the urgency and desire in her eyes, he slowly shook his head while his breathing quickened, and his body hardened. Her scent filled his senses and the need to take her soft body in his arms was irresistible. She was so lovely, but troubled, as she tried to come to terms with finding Lady Anne and losing her again, he longed to comfort her any way he could.

She saw his indecision and her dark-blue eyes widened, filled with passionate desire. Leaning close, she traced the line of his jaw with a slender finger. "I intended to take a lover before I marry. Even before I met you, Damian."

So, if not him, then some other man, who might not treat her well. Jealousy seared through him like fire at the thought of her in someone else's arms, some rake kissing her, taking pleasure in her body. *No!*

As the coach bumped along the road, he lowered the carriage blinds. Damian didn't fool himself into believing he would stop after a few kisses, but she would remain a virgin when he left her. He refused to risk her becoming pregnant. With a sharp intake of breath, he cupped her chin and ran a thumb over her trembling full lip, then with a moan, pressed his mouth to hers.

Chapter Sixteen

T HE BREEZE THROUGH the open window stirred the blinds and cool air drifted over Diana's heated skin. Once her breasts were freed from her bodice, Ballantine had tweaked and kissed her nipples into hard, sensitive peaks, making her whimper and wriggle and sigh.

"Damian, do people really do such things?" she whispered, shocked, when he eased up her skirts and kneeled to settle between her legs.

He gazed up at her, breathing fast, his eyes heavy lidded. "They do, sweetheart, with alacrity."

While she wanted him to pleasure her, the very notion of something so intimate was beyond her imagining. Society's expectations of how a lady must behave had rarely bothered her, but still…a moan fractured her thoughts. Had it come from her? She licked her lips swollen from his kisses and grasped fistfuls of his silky, dark-brown hair sliding through her fingers. With incoherent murmurs, she lost herself in the sweet ecstasy, her embarrassment turning to breathless need.

"Leave me some hair, please, sweetheart."

Ballantine's warm breath feathered over her skin, his voice a deep rumble. "Like cream silk." The warmth of his breath was exciting against her soft skin as he pressed his mouth to her inner thigh. His fingers stroked her slick skin, and he pushed a finger inside her. Her stomach and thighs tightened, and she cried out at the rolling explosion of feeling before all thoughts left her in a melting of muscle and bone.

He shushed her with his mouth on hers. Their panting breaths filled the carriage. He groaned, then murmured in her ear something she couldn't quite make out. *I must ask him afterward,* she thought. But after he'd delicately bitten her earlobe and planted small kisses along her collarbone, she forgot.

Ballantine breathed heavily as he sat beside her and pulled her to him, his hand cradling her hair. In a state of pure bliss, she curled up against him as her breath slowed and laid her head against his warm chest, listening to the fast beating of his heart. Guilt tugged at her. The hard ridge in his pantaloons pressed against her thigh. Of course he wanted her, but he made no move to act on it. She yearned to touch him there, to lie down with his heavy weight upon her, to have him inside her. Diana swiveled to look up at him. "Can't I touch you?"

For a moment, he didn't answer. "That wouldn't be wise, Diana."

"But we didn't... You didn't..."

"No, sweetheart," he said, his voice warm.

"It was lovely..." But it had only made her want more. She was greedy for him. She knew there was more—she had found a book of lurid drawings in her father's library. Up on the top shelf, where he must have thought she couldn't reach. Her face had burned as she'd turned the pages, and her heart had raced.

Frustrated, Diana tucked her bodice into place and eased her skirts down over her trembling thighs. "I expected us to..."

"Not in a carriage. Not your first time. You deserve better."

She doubted it could ever be better. Especially with anyone else.

"While making the beast with two backs, to quote Shakespeare, is devoutly to be wished, rushing it, and here, would be a travesty." He stroked her arm. "Nothing will equal lying in your marriage bed with your husband and pleasuring each other for many hours."

She thrust away the image of him naked in her bed while he helped her into her pelisse. Buttoning it to the neck, she snatched up her bonnet. "That would depend on the husband," she said crisply, so disappointed, she thought she might cry. Had being with her pleased him at all?

He put his hands on her shoulders to steady her fumbling fingers and tied the ribbons of her bonnet beneath her chin. "We must be nearing the outskirts of Combe Down."

"But, Ballantine, you received no enjoyment from this."

He raised an amused eyebrow. "I enjoyed it immensely, and I thank you for the privilege." He lifted her onto his lap, kissed her deeply, pulling her close, making her giddy and restless with the hard length of his maleness and the scent of herself upon him. Did he wish the future could be different? That they might be together? Or was she just another woman in his life? A naïve one, at that.

She must get control of herself. Ballantine wasn't the prince who would one day come to claim her and snatch her away from the villain.

Ballantine settled back on the opposite seat and raised the blinds. Moments later, the carriage pulled up outside Tims's home.

Diana tugged on her gloves. "Finding Anne for me has brought me peace. You have been everything I wished for and more, Ballantine."

His eyes looked sad as he scrutinized her face. As if it might be the last time he saw her. "You've been everything I knew you would be, sweetheart. I will miss you very much."

She had hoped he'd say he loved her but didn't expect it. Nor would he want to hear her declaration of love. "I won't forget you, or what we shared. Never."

"Oh, you will in time. Once you marry."

She caught her breath at the sudden, stark pain in his eyes.

Tims hurried out of the cottage with her bag. Once she'd

settled in the carriage, it put an end to any further intimacy between her and Damian.

The maid's eyes widened as she looked from Diana to Damian, then she ducked her head to examine her reticule.

The countryside swept past the window, and within the hour, a few small cottages were replaced with noisy, bustling streets and larger buildings as they threaded their way through the increasingly heavy traffic, the air now filled with the smell of smoke and horse manure. The carriage was taking her to her destination and him away from her. *Forever?* She blinked as tears hovered hot behind her lids. He must not see them.

"Ballantine..." The carriage juddered to a stop a few townhouses away from the Howards'. The groom jumped down, opened the door, and lowered the steps. Ballantine shook his head to silence her, then left the carriage to assist her and Tims to the footpath. Diana stood, her legs a little shaky, while she took her portmanteau from the groom.

With a brief nod of farewell, Ballantine leaped inside the carriage once more, and the door closed. The coachman ordered the horses to walk on, and the carriage proceeded down the road. Diana watched it until it was out of sight and tried to pull herself together. Then she turned and hurried up the street to Penny's parents' townhouse, with Tims following. Would what had occurred between her and Ballantine show on her face? She was no longer the young innocent, whatever Ballantine had said. She thought differently. Saw the world differently. And her heart throbbed as if it would break. It would be difficult to hide such a monumental change in her. Would Penny sense it?

Her steps faltered, then with a deep breath of the cool, Bath air, she firmed her shoulders and walked on.

At the top of the three-story townhouse steps, she rapped on the brass knocker. The Howards' footman opened it.

"Lady Diana?" The butler, a man of late middle years with grizzled hair, greeted her at the door. He looked puzzled as he glanced up and down the street. "I didn't hear the coach." He smiled. "It is good to see you again."

Diana returned his smile. "It is an age since I last visited. I hope you are well, Laycock?"

"I am indeed, thank you, Lady Diana." He snapped his fingers, and the footman hurried to take her things. "Miss Penelope is in the morning room with her mother. Perhaps you would prefer to remove the travel dust after your journey before you join them?"

"Yes, I would. Thank you."

Relishing a few quiet moments alone to compose herself before Penny bombarded her with questions, Diana and Tims followed the housekeeper up the stairs. Her thoughts returned swiftly to Ballantine. What an accomplished lover he was. Her body felt alive, as if it had awakened from a long sleep. Tims, although obviously bursting with curiosity, remained silent as she unpacked Diana's bag, and when a household servant brought hot water, Diana washed herself and had Tims tidy her hair. She had brought very few clothes with her, and they were a little crumpled, which no doubt Penny's mother would notice.

Diana was gazing with concern at her wrinkled morning gown when the door opened, and Penny rushed in. "You're here at last! I confess to being on tenterhooks worrying about you. Quickly, tell me all! We must get our story straight before you go down to Mama. Fortunately, she has a visitor and won't notice my absence for a while." She glanced at Tims. "Send your maid down to the servants' hall for tea. I'll have mine iron that dress."

While Penny's maid ironed Diana's gown in the adjoining dressing room, Diana told Penny a little of what had happened, while omitting Anne's new name or where she lived. She also left off the last part with Damian, which still made her blush.

"We must keep this to ourselves," Diana said. "Do not breathe a word of it. It would be utter disaster should Anne's father hear of it."

"I promise. Fancy! Anne!" Penny grinned. "I never would have believed it of her. But I am so glad she is well and happy."

"Yes. I shall miss her," Diana said gravely.

"You may see her again. You never know. When you're married, your husband might take you there."

"I shall never tell another soul about Anne. Nor must you, Penny. It could be dangerous for her."

Penny nodded, subdued. "Yes. I can understand that." She looked at Diana with concern in her eyes. "I haven't told you! The duke sent a footman with a message yesterday. Fortunately, I wrestled it from Laycock before he could deliver it to Mama. We can rely on Laycock's discretion, never fear!"

"What did the missive say?" Diana asked impatiently.

"Only that your father's coach will collect you tomorrow. Your presence is required at home."

"Tomorrow? Why so soon?" Diana murmured uneasily. Did her father have some plan for her? Or had he discovered she hadn't been in Bath?

>>>×<<<

IT HAD FELT so right for them to be together. Damian could usually rely on his ability to keep control of his emotions, but he'd come close to losing it, to tossing his good sense to the wind with the urgent need to make her his. He sighed and leaned back against the squab. On many levels, that would be wrong. He must move on, concentrate on what lay ahead for him in France. And trust Diana would find contentment in her life without him.

He tried to thrust away the taste of her, the touch of silky skin, molding her soft breasts in his hands, the strawberry colored nipples firming under his touch, the scent of aroused woman. He had told her he was privileged, and indeed he had been.

It had begun to rain heavily, the air misty, when very late in the evening, having remained alert with his gun at his side for the long journey home, he stretched his back as he walked from the stables to the front door, passing the library windows ablaze with candlelight. He used his key to enter and found the footman dozing on his chair in the grand hall. "Sleeping on the job, William?"

The young man jumped to his feet, blushed fiercely, and bowed. "Milord."

Damian chuckled as he removed his hat and gloves. "I imagine Mrs. Mowbray has retired for the evening. Have the kitchen staff rustle me up some food. Something cold from the pantry will do. I'll be in the library, where I trust I'll find my brother?"

"Yes, milord."

Damian strode along the corridor.

"*Woof!*" When he opened the door, his red setter, Max, greeted him, his paws resting on Damian's chest almost pushing him backward.

"Steady, boy." He grinned, rubbing the dog's silky fur.

"I must confess to having tried to turn his affections toward me," Luke said, lazing on the sofa with a book. "But he remains loyal to you, though I cannot imagine why. You are the most casual of masters."

"Max knows the true meaning of loyalty." Damian's mouth quirked with amusement. Pleased to be in his favorite room, the rows of book-laden wooden shelves smelling of beeswax and hide-bound volumes, with a hint of dust and mold. He crossed the brightly colored Persian rugs covering the wooden floors and sat in the highbacked wingchair opposite Luke, close to a small, coal fire smoldering in the grate of the marble fireplace. He studied his brother's face. "You look remarkably well," he said, reassured.

"I ache in places I wasn't aware of," Luke said ruefully. "Took a couple of workers to help a neighbor with his drainage."

"Who was it?"

"Old Kemble. He looks frail, but I hate to admit he put me to shame."

Damian laughed. "He's a splendid fellow."

"So is Mrs. Kemble, who plied me with delicious pastries and cups of tea." Luke's smile faded. "You, however, do not look in the pink. Might I ask how it went with the lady?"

Damian stretched his legs out to the fire, feeling the welcome heat from the smoldering coal. "Well, I'm pleased to say."

Luke nodded. "And the lady showed her gratitude?"

Damian frowned and smoothed back his hair with both hands. "She is not a lightskirt, Luke, but a lady. I was glad to help her."

Luke gazed at him thoughtfully. "And came away a little bruised, I suspect."

"Perhaps. Let's speak of other things."

The footman brought in a tray with ham pie, bread and butter, and one of Cook's special puddings. Damian rubbed his hands. "Ah, I'm ravenous. Fetch me a glass of that claret on the sideboard, Luke, and tell me how things stand here. What did the bailiff have to say about the last sitting of the Assizes?"

Some hours later, Damian settled into bed. He found sleep elusive, his mind dwelling on his last moments alone with Diana. It would not be so easy to pick up the threads of his life now after what had happened between them.

The next morning, after breakfast, Damian rode over the estate with Luke, Max following at the horses' heels, relishing the familiar scents of trees and grasses, and the dank smell of the river. When he returned to the house he found his orders had arrived. He was to liaise with British spies in a small village on the French coast and make his way to Paris. The British intelligence officer, Colquhoun Grant, who had been posted on the Iberian Peninsula under the command of Arthur Wellesley, had been captured by the French. In full uniform, he had been treated as a fellow officer and sent to Paris, where he secretly sent and received messages from captivity. Suspected of spying, Marshal Auguste de Marmont refused to swap him for a French prisoner, keeping him there for interrogation.

Damian's mission was to join some Englishmen to aid in Grant's escape. He had his bag packed for France.

About to enter the carriage bound for the Horse Guards, Luke stood on the drive, Max sitting beside him, tongue lolling. Luke assured Damian he was not to spare a thought either about the estate or him.

Damian grinned. "I hadn't intended to."

"But you would have, anyway," Luke said. "I haven't told you about the improvements to my social life."

Damian paused on the step. "Oh? And you tell me now?"

"To avoid any degree of interrogation," his annoying brother said. "I have attended some assemblies. Dined with neighbors and met some interesting people."

"Any of the female variety?"

Luke looked evasive. "One or two."

"Ah." Damian nodded.

"Best not keep the horses standing." Luke stepped back and smiled at him. "Stay safe, brother. Don't be a hero."

As the carriage continued down the drive, Damian turned to glance back. He felt heartened by Luke's news. It appeared, although still cautiously guarding his heart, that his brother was finally coming to terms with his tragic past. What would the future hold for him? Or either of them, for that matter. Damian would sail on the tide, and this was the most dangerous mission he had ever undertaken.

Chapter Seventeen

B Y THE TIME the carriage had drawn up outside Diana's home, she was in a fever of expectation. A disturbing monologue kept running through her head. Was her father angry? Had he become aware of her deceit? She doubted he would hear of it from her loyal maid, Tims, who kept her secrets. And Diana had sworn the coachman, groom, and footman to secrecy when they had left Tims at her parents' home and dropped off Diana alone before her meeting with Damian. The coachman and footman knew her well, the two of them having been in her father's employ for some years, and she was sure at least two of them would keep her secret, but she was not sure of their new groom, Peter.

Diana should have been ashamed to have gone behind her father's back, but she wasn't. She had found Anne, and her dear friend was happy. And that meant a great deal to her, even though she must never speak of it.

Those precious hours alone with Ballantine she would hold forever in her heart.

Anticipating the worrying scene with her father, Diana sighed deeply as she walked along the corridor to his studio and knocked on the door.

"Come."

Diana entered, finding him alone, sketching at his easel. "You sent for me, Papa?"

He swiveled on his stool and cast a baleful eye over her, then beckoned her closer.

She hurried across the rug and kissed his cheek, breathing in his familiar lemony shaving soap blending into the room with the usual smells of turpentine and oil paint. He looked tired, the grooves beside his mouth deeper than she remembered. Struggling with a guilty conscience and sympathy, she could only hope his tiredness was due to his working late by candlelight and not worry about her.

"You left your maid with her family in Combe Down and traveled on without her? Why?"

"She wished to visit her mother," Diana said. "She joined me at Penny's soon afterward."

"It appears I must watch everything you do more closely. You're too old for a governess. Must I employ a companion for you? Some widow of good sense to accompany you everywhere?"

Peter had betrayed her. Dismay at a possible end to her freedom tightened her stomach. "Tims hasn't seen her mother all year," Diana said, which at least was the truth.

"What mischief did you get up to without your maid? Never mind, don't tell me. It is of no consequence now." Dismissing her with a wave of his charcoal, he turned back to his drawing. It was of a tree by a river, with a humble cottage perched near the bank. Not a naked woman in sight.

"I like this one very much," she said, moving closer to inspect it. "You so seldom paint a landscape."

"There's a mood for it, that and portraits. But I have no desire to paint clients." He chuckled, his charcoal tracing the limbs of a stately oak. "Lady Belfries wished to commission me to paint her portrait. She would not have cared for the result because I would have included that wart on her chin."

Diana giggled.

He turned to observe her. "It is good to have you home. The place seems to echo when you're gone. Never noticed it before.

Perhaps I should marry again," he said, more to himself than her. "But I've met no one to equal your mother."

Diana stared him in surprise. She'd thought her father hadn't cared very much for her mother. Had he told Mama that? She hoped so, and often, because she had loved him until her last breath.

"But everything is about to change, as you will soon be married," he added.

Her heart beating like a trapped bird's wings, Diana waited for him to continue.

Papa left his stool and gestured to the sofa. "Sit down. I wish to speak to you."

She joined him, trying to breathe normally, fearing what was to come. Who was this man she must marry?

"Lord Montgomery has asked for your hand."

Diana's mouth fell open. "Lord Montgomery? Haven't you already refused him?"

"He approached me again. I have reviewed his proposal and see no reason to reject it. He is an upstanding fellow with good connections." He raised his dark eyebrows. "You can hardly disapprove of his appearance."

Diana's heart pounded in her ears. She fought not to tremble. "He's not a nice man," she said. "I found his manner toward me insulting."

He frowned. "The same old excuses. I expected you to object, and I'm weary of it, Diana. Many would say I've been far too lenient with you. I'm prepared to allow a reasonable time for your courtship. We will return to London and spend a month there, where you can see more of the fellow to get to know him." He stood. "I believe you will change your mind about him in time. But get used to the idea. You have enjoyed too much freedom here. You ride around like a hoyden with no mother to teach you how a young lady should behave. If I don't act now, something bad could befall you. And I prefer to hand you over to a strong man to take care of you. I shan't be swayed from my purpose again."

Diana left the studio. She ran up to her bedchamber and threw herself on her bed. She lay staring up at the swath of rose-pink damask overhead on the canopy. Why did Lord Montgomery wish to marry her? He must have been aware of how little regard she had for him. It unnerved her to think of their last conversation when he'd abandoned any pretense at politeness. And then he'd tried to make amends, in the belief that she would forgive him. What it *had* done was give her a glimpse into his dark soul. He frightened her. She couldn't marry him. He was so arrogant and confident of his status in society, he felt he could treat her as he wished. She'd rather run away than marry him. As Anne had done. A shudder passed through her, and she wrapped her arms around herself. Running away was impossible. Diana had no one to aid her. She couldn't do that to Penny or Anne. Ballantine was the one man who might agree to help her, although she doubted he'd approve. But he was gone from her life, she thought sadly.

She sat up. Grandmama would wish to help her, but she had spoken against Lord Montgomery before and that hadn't changed Papa's mind. She rang for Tims while she clung to the hope that something would happen to prevent the marriage in the time left to her.

WITHIN DAYS, DIANA was again in London, staying with her grandmother in her Mayfair townhouse. When she'd told her about Lord Montgomery, Grandmama had become angry but had fallen short of criticizing her son too harshly. "Never fear. There's many a slip between cup and lip," she'd said enigmatically. Diana wished that had made her feel better, but it had failed to.

The previous Wednesday, she and Lord Montgomery had

danced at Almack's. Spying the triumphant gleam in his eyes, she'd come away fearing him even more. Ballantine had not attended. She hadn't really expected to find him there. Almack's was not the sort of venue he would go to when most who frequented it searched for a husband or wife. He had also been absent from the ball on the following Saturday, and a card party on Monday. It cast her into gloom, but when she thought about it, he could do nothing to save her from Lord Montgomery— except ask for her hand. And he had made it clear he had no intention of doing that. It would have been inappropriate and perhaps unwelcome to seek his advice or his sympathy, so it was fortunate he was not present to tempt her.

Tonight in the Inglebys' ballroom it was good to be among people again, and she felt quite lighthearted with relief that Lord Montgomery had not approached her. But she sensed him watching her while she danced a quadrille from where he stood among the guests on the fringe of the ballroom.

Perhaps he disliked the idea of meeting her grandmother again. Grandmama didn't trouble herself to engage in polite conversation with him, which left him looking uncomfortable. "I am at an age to please myself whom I speak to," she had told Diana earlier. "And I don't wish to talk to him. Should you be married to Lord Montgomery, I would make an effort."

Diana had gazed at her, horrified. "But I shan't marry him. I'd rather die."

Grandmama had patted her hand. "Such dramatics. I didn't say you *would* marry him. Have patience, Diana."

Patience? It had never been her strong suit and was in short supply now.

IT WAS CLOSE to dawn. After forging the storm-driven waves of the Channel for more hours than Damian cared for, flickering lights from the French landscape shrouded by the dark night were welcome. While under the cover of a deep bank of clouds, the ship moored off the coast. A few miles from Le Havre, his companions rowed to shore in a quiet bay. Wading through the shallows, he reached the gritty sand and pebbles in search of any sign of movement. As the lavender-gray dawn lightened the sky, trees and rooftops came into view.

A low whistle came from the deep-purple shadows. Two quick bursts, a break of silence, then one more. Damian replied in kind. Two men appeared at a run and crossed the shore to him. They exchanged the secret password.

"Beau," Damian said, offering his hand to the tall, rangy fellow with the bushy, red beard.

He shook it vigorously. "Pole, sir. Ye are too late to rescue Grant. He left our shores some hours ago on his way to join Wellesley."

Damian bent and brushed the sand from his boots and breeches. "Grant is safely away? Excellent news. I should like to thank the man responsible for his escape. Is he here among you?"

"Unfortunately, he is not. It was an Englishman by the name of Crow who got Grant out of Paris," Pole said.

Damian nodded, recognizing the alias of the clever intelligence officer Giles Devereux, Earl of Halcrow. They had crossed paths before while involved in this business. "Then I'll board the next vessel back to England." He paused. "Did Crow go with Grant on the boat?"

"No, sir. The French captured him. They hold him prisoner."

Damian cursed. "Bloody hell! Do you know where they keep him?"

"We do, sir, although not much good it does us. The camp isn't far, about fifteen miles as the crow flies, but it's impossible to get Crow out. We heard Marshal Auguste de Marmont is livid, as he hoped to discover more about Wellesley's plans from Grant. Little did he know Grant ran an intelligence service for Wellesley, sending and receiving letters from within the heart of Paris. Now, with Grant escaping from under his nose, he is intent on making an example of Crow, who is closely guarded. It's like a fortress and crawling with Bonaparte's men."

Damian was not about to leave Giles to be shot as a traitor without doing his best to get him out. "Can you show me exactly where this monastery is situated?"

"If you'll come with us, Beau, I will draw a map for you. We can supply you with arms, food, and a fresh mount, but I am the only one able to accompany you. And am pleased to do it."

Damian nodded, his smile grim. "I am glad to have you with me. Lead the way to your hideout."

While they waited for the cover of darkness, Damian learned what he could from Pole, the man in charge, who drew a crude map. "At the behest of de Marmont, a unit of his men have occupied a Gothic monastery overlooking the River Seine near the town of Les Andelys. Sentries patrol the grounds, and the back of the building can only be reached by fording the river."

"If you can furnish me with a boat, I'll find a way in," Damian said.

"We might steal one. There are always a few fishing boats and rowing boats moored upriver, closer to the town," Pole said. "But once you cross, if you can manage it undetected, you must find where they hold Crow. My guess is in the dungeons." He shook his head and raised his hands in a gesture of helplessness. "So you must realize what an impossible task it will be to reach him, let alone get him away alive."

Damian nodded gravely as he munched through bread and cheese. "I do."

"So you'll not tackle it?" Pole's grimace expressed his regret.

He could not walk away like a coward and live with his conscience. "Of course I will. And should I succeed, can you have your men meet us on the road somewhere closer to the coast and get us on a boat?"

Pole's eyes lit up. "That, we can do." He named a village and showed Damian where it was on the map.

Damian took a swig of ale. "Right. If we leave at dusk, we'll arrive about midnight?"

"As near as dammit, sir," Pole said.

Damian put down the mug and leaned back, resting his feet on a spare chair. "Please wake me when it's time to leave, Pole."

"Right you are, Beau."

Pole's sturdy frame slipped away surprisingly silently and fleet of foot. Beyond the window of the cottage on the outskirts of a small village, the wind whispered through the trees and ducks and chickens squawked around the yard. Men's voices drifted from where they gathered together, smoking their pipes. Damian breathed in dust, hay, hops, and the rancid smell of men's sweat as he closed his eyes. He had trained himself to kip whenever he could during a mission. Despite this one proving to be treacherous and a serious challenge, he had no trouble drifting off.

Chapter Eighteen

"YOU ARE PLEASING to the eye tonight, Lady Diana." Amusement tugged at Lord Montgomery's fleshy lips but failed to reach his eyes. "Once you stop glaring at me."

Unsettled, she steadied herself as they danced the waltz. "Have I stopped, sir? I wasn't aware of it."

With a smile for the benefit of the surrounding dancers, he leaned closer, and she saw she'd riled him. "You are determined to make this betrothal as difficult as you can, aren't you? It would not go well for you should I complain to your father."

"You know my feelings on the matter, sir." Diana longed to break away from him. His sly face invited a good slap. "Why do you wish to marry me?"

"You seem unaware of your attractions, Lady Diana." His hand tightened at her waist. "But I fancy a firebrand for a wife. I'll enjoy the challenge."

Diana dragged in a breath so deep and fast, a wave of dizziness passed over her. She feared she'd lose her balance. It would be preferable to fall in a heap at his feet rather than cling to him for support. Fortunately, her head cleared, her anger warming her. "You will never bend me to your will, sir. Your life will be a misery, I promise you."

His eyes turned flinty. "You will learn not to cross me," he murmured as Mrs. Bell swept past on Lord Truedale's arm. Lord

Montgomery nodded to them before he turned back to Diana. "I'm reminded of a stallion I once owned. He had wanted his freedom too." His tight-lipped smile was for the *ton*'s benefit, but the chilling look in his eyes reminded her of frost on a stone statue in the garden. "Until I persuaded him otherwise with the use of the whip."

Diana tried to pull her hand away from his hard grasp. "When I tell my father about this, it will put an end to your objectives."

"The duke won't believe you. He confesses to being out of patience with you. Apparently, you have contrived to find reasons not to marry in the past."

She feared he was right about Papa. Unable to deal with any more of Lord Montgomery's vitriol, she wanted to break away and leave him standing there alone. Not caring if she made a fool of herself as well as him. But before she could act, the dance came to an end. As if he could read her thoughts, his hand fastened on hers in an iron grip as he led her from the floor. Then, with a bow to her grandmother, he left them.

Grandmama gazed at her with concern. "Lord Montgomery looked furious, and I see you are distraught." She gathered up her things and rose, gesturing to a passing footman. "We are leaving. Please advise the duke. You might find him in the gaming room."

"Certainly, my lady." The footman bowed. "I'll send for your carriage."

Diana felt Lord Montgomery's angry gaze burning into her back as they left the ballroom, but she refused to glance his way. Let all the world think she'd snubbed him. She sagged against the squab as the carriage took them home. It was possible Lord Montgomery would tell her father about how she'd spoken to him. The man wasn't bound by any sense of honor and didn't care a whisker about her. It became urgent that she discover something about him which would force Papa to refuse him. But who could she turn to for help? Ballantine had disliked the idea of her marriage when she had surmised Lord Montgomery had first raised it with her father. And he would know more about the viscount. She knew she had promised she would never ask him for anything again, but she felt confident that if he learned of her plight, he would help her.

She would write as soon as she arrived home and address a letter to his town address and another to his country estate, where he might still be spending time with his brother. She couldn't allow herself to think he might have gone on some dangerous mission.

"You look too pale. Come to the parlor and have a hot drink before you retire," Grandmama said when the carriage stopped before her house. "I wish to talk to you."

Diana followed her. The icy knot in her chest made the drink welcome, but she was unsure how much she should tell her grandmother. To repeat what Lord Montgomery had said would upset her, and Diana was impatient to go up to her chamber and write the letters. But, settled by the fire sipping hot chocolate, her angst eased a little as the distress at Lord Montgomery's behavior and the chill of the evening left her.

Grandmama stroked the gray tabby which had left his basket to climb onto her lap. "Now, my dear child. Tell me what that man said to upset you."

"Lord Montgomery believes I need more discipline. He intends to teach me how to become a submissive wife."

Grandmama's eyes narrowed. "Does he, indeed."

"Should Papa be told?" Diana asked hopefully.

"No. Lord Montgomery would only offer a different version of events. Leave it with me, child. I shall give it some thought."

She finished her chocolate and kissed her grandmother's soft, perfumed cheek. Once she'd climbed into bed, she gazed sleeplessly into the dark. Could Grandmama change Papa's mind? Diana couldn't make herself believe it. Papa had taken notice of his mother's advice before, but not about this. He believed it to be the right decision, and knowledge of their engagement had already spread through the *ton*. Papa seldom worried about causing a scandal. He seemed to sail above them unscathed, but he wouldn't want to appear a fool by suddenly changing his mind and refusing the viscount twice.

Although Diana had promised not to ask Ballantine for help again, she would send the letters first thing in the morning. They had shared a dislike of Lord Montgomery when at Holland House. He might know something that wasn't common knowledge. A man such as Lord Montgomery must have an unsavory past.

Rising early with the letters clutched in her shaky fingers, Diana went downstairs. She handed them to a footman in the hall to post. In the breakfast room, inviting aromas of bacon, eggs, and kippers made her realize she'd barely eaten since luncheon yesterday. Perhaps food would help to make her calmer.

Her grandmother entered as Diana sipped her tea. Grandmama rarely rose before noon after they'd attended a ball. She looked thoughtful as she sat down but offered no insight into Diana's plight. Diana despairingly poked at her eggs with her fork, her appetite waning.

The following two days seemed endless, despite the shopping trips to purchase a fan and feathers to dress Grandmama's favorite bonnet, plus the last visit to the modiste for a walking gown for Diana to wear while promenading in Hyde Park. It now resided in its box with sheets of tissue paper for Tims to deal with. Normally, a new gown gave Diana pleasure, but not now. All the joy seemed to have seeped out of her life.

As the next morning dawned fine, she and Grandmama ambled along the shady paths of Hyde Park. She watched the horse riders in Rotten Row with envy, longing to be among them. But her father, still unhappy with her, had not seen fit to hire a horse for her.

She had not seen Lord Montgomery since the ball when he had mentioned calling to invite her for a drive in the park. Dare she hope he'd changed his mind? What man would want a wife who so obviously disliked him? His true motives were difficult to fathom, but she suspected marrying into a revered family such as the Staffords suited him. Her stomach roiled to think he'd meant it when he'd said he wished to break her will.

Grandmama had been silent on the subject and Diana hadn't mentioned it again. Diana inspected the post as soon as it arrived, waiting impatiently for Ballantine's reply.

On the fourth day, a letter came. Diana practically snatched it from the footman and hurried into the morning room to read it. She moaned with disappointment. It came not from Ballantine, but from his brother, Mr. Beaufort. When Lord Ballantine's secretary had drawn his attention to her letter, Mr. Beaufort wrote, he'd felt obliged to advise her of his brother's absence from the country.

Ballantine isn't in England? Her worst fears realized, she shivered and rubbed her arms. Did this mean Ballantine was in danger? He must have still been alive. Like with Anne, she would know if he wasn't. Diana curled up on the sofa, the letter clutched in her hand. Was there nothing to be done?

⟫⟫⟫⟫✕⟪⟪⟪⟪

As DUSK APPROACHED, Pole, the man who was proving to be invaluable to Damian, gathered his men around him in the cottage garden.

"While I don't intend to ask any of you to embark on the impossible mission Beau here intends to tackle, there might be one of you with knowledge of Les Andelys and the monastery beside the Seine, where the French hold an Englishman." Pole turned to a thin, young man of about eighteen years with a shock of black hair. "Bart? Your family hails from those parts, do they not?"

Bart shuffled forward over the grass. He scowled. "My *oncle* lived there until he went to Paris to sell cabbages from his farm. Grabbed off a street he was and found himself in Bonaparte's army. Dead within a month." He spat out the words, trembling with anger.

Damian drew Bart away to a quiet corner near the chicken coop. "We need to hear what you know, Bart," he said.

"*Oncle* told me of a tunnel. The monks at the abbey used it to escape during the Terror when angry mobs and revolutionaries began attacking them. I don't know if it still exists."

Hope caused a burst of energy to race through Damian's veins. Getting Halcrow out might be possible, and with his own skin intact. "Will you show me the entrance to this tunnel? I'll ask no more of you."

Bart's boyish face drooped, and panic turned his brown eyes black. "I never go there, sir, not since my *tante* died. Too dangerous in those parts."

Damian took two gold sovereigns from his pocket and tossed one to Bart. "One now, and the other when we find the entrance."

Bart hungrily eyed the coin as if it burned in his palm. His fingers closed around it, and he nodded.

Pole glanced up at the darkening sky. "We need to leave." He turned and yelled at one of his men. "Bring the trap round. And Lucifer, for Beau to ride."

Damian's heart sank as he viewed the skinny, old animal. As he mounted, he hoped it would last the distance, wishing he could set it free to spend its last days in a lush meadow where it could eat its fill.

Through the long twilight, Damian rode out the gate onto the lane with Pole and Bart ahead of him in the trap. The golden glow vanished from the landscape as in the west, the sun dipped below the horizon, the air still warm. He hoped for a moon to light their way. A lantern swung from the trap but would have to be doused before they reached the abbey.

It was about an hour before midnight when, hidden from the abbey by trees, they approached the graveyard where Bart said the entrance to the tunnel would be found. It wasn't enough to hang his hopes on, Damian realized, but there was nothing else.

Dismounting, his senses on high alert, he followed young Bart through what seemed little more than a pile of broken stones. The sliver of a moon sailed high in the sky, bathing the few headstones still standing in a faint, silvery light. Apart from the roar of the river and an occasional bird call, the world seemed hushed, as if the violence perpetrated by war hadn't touched here, although it lurked behind the stone abbey walls. Damian's stomach tightened, and he prayed he wasn't too late to find Crow alive.

With Pole, he followed Bart over the flagstones across a thick mat of grass and weeds that tried to trip him. Purple Shadows stretched across the dank-smelling grounds, dark and foreboding. One might have imagined ghosts hovering about, but Damian did not believe in ghosts. He focused on the bulky outline of the abbey rising above that copse of trees, where he knew the guards would wait, alert to any intruder.

Bart disappeared into what appeared to be a dark well. He emerged again within minutes. "It's not boarded up from the outside."

"Good lad." Damian descended the slippery, moss-covered steps, then came to what appeared to be a solid wall. Following Bart's directions, he felt his way along, then came to wood: a small, arched door rough beneath his fingers, completely hidden behind a large bush.

He tried to open it, but it was stuck fast. "I pray they haven't blocked it up inside, or the tunnel hasn't caved in. Let's put our shoulders to the door."

Pole came down and the three men heaved. With a groan loud enough to wake the dead, the door creaked as it slowly opened, and the dust of the ages wafted out in a choking cloud along with the stench of rats.

Damian climbed back up the steps. "I'll go on alone. Thank you, Bart." He fished the sovereign out of his pocket, handing it to Bart, who scurried away as if the hounds of hell were chasing him.

"My thanks to you, Pole. I hope to find you waiting with a vehicle, at the place you pointed out near the willows. If we don't show up before daylight, leave. I see no reason for de Marmont's men to capture more of us."

"I'll be there, Beau," Pole said. "And have a rowboat waiting to row you out to the fishing boat. They'll drop you somewhere on the English coast. Lucifer doesn't look like much, but he'll carry the two of you. He's done it before."

Damian eyed the old, brown horse doubtfully where the animal pulled at the grass. "I appreciate it."

"*Bonne chance*," came the whispered reply, and Pole was gone, back to where he left the trap.

Damian went back down the steps, wondering what he'd face inside. And whether he'd ever see the light of day again.

Chapter Nineteen

DIANA FRETTED THROUGH another day. Ill with worry, she begged her grandmother to refuse an invitation that evening to the Johnsons' card party. Lord Montgomery was sure to be there. He might endeavor to speak to her alone. To frighten her with more of his threats when she refused to become the submissive, young miss he intended for a wife. She knew herself too well. There would be a horrible scene. How disappointed Papa would be in her! He'd be even more convinced she should marry as soon as possible. Her freedom and her future were at stake; she must act. But what could she do?

As she lay in bed with a cold compress on her aching forehead, Grandmama came to sit beside her. "How are you, Diana? Feeling better?"

"A little, Grandmama."

"I have ordered a tincture. It might settle your stomach."

Diana screwed up her nose. "Thank you."

Smiling, her grandmother smoothed her blankets. "You shall feel better in no time. You look far too well to be an invalid."

"Grandmama…"

She held up her hand. "I know what troubles you. And I shan't stand by and watch your life ruined. I recall Lady Slade mentioning Lord Montgomery asked her daughter, Felicity, to marry him at one time. They rejected his proposal. I have written to her in Devon to ask why. We shall see what they have to say about him."

"Oh, that is an excellent idea, Grandmama." Diana squeezed her thin hand. "It gives me hope."

But when her grandmother left her, her head sank back on the pillow. It was unlikely anything Lady Slade's daughter could say would change her father's mind. She must find an answer herself. Perhaps she could trick Lord Montgomery into revealing his true nature within her father's hearing. She closed her eyes and considered how it might be done.

The following day, with a plan in mind to prevent the wedding, Diana felt better as she came downstairs for luncheon. She found her father in the dining room buttering bread, a joint of ham, bread, and salad on the table before him.

"There you are. Your grandmother tells me you have been unwell. Are you feeling better now?"

"Yes, Papa." She took a breath. "I thought perhaps…"

"Sit down and have something to eat. You look too pale." He smiled. "Lord Montgomery has requested we bring the wedding date forward, and I have agreed. The ceremony is to be held in the chapel at Ashburnham Hall in three weeks' time. I have ordered my secretary to arrange for invitations to be sent and a notice placed in the morning newspapers. Your grandmama will assist with your trousseau." His gaze dared her to argue. "That should give you adequate time to prepare, Diana. You may have an attendant if you wish and all the trimmings you desire." He took a bite of the bread and ham and chewed thoughtfully as she slumped in her chair. "You will come to see the sense of this," he said, leaving her speechless.

It was too late for Grandmama to do anything to prevent it. Too late for Ballantine to help. She lowered her head and bit her lip, having lost the will to argue.

IT WAS DARKER than midnight inside the tunnel, and airless. Damian took a rushlight from his pocket and struck a flint against the stone wall. A flickering flame caught the tallow-soaked rush. The feeble glow revealed the ceiling of stone, not far above his head, and walls that seemed to close in on him. At the far end of the tunnel, a short flight of steps led upward. He climbed them and stood before the oak door at the top, wondering what he'd find should he go through it. Was he about to make his presence known to the guards? No sound penetrated the solid, old abbey walls. With a deep breath, he grasped the brass latch and eased the door open, praying it wouldn't groan. When it opened smoothly, he feared it might be in use. Did they know about the tunnel and had set a trap for the unwary? He had no answer to those questions that flooded his mind, so he pushed the door wider and stepped into a tiny room.

Holding the rushlight aloft, he found it was a storeroom, the shelves stacked with urns, pottery, wooden utensils, and metal plates. He opened the door and stepped out into breathless silence. The room he found himself in was a cavernous space stacked with wine barrels. Smelling smoke, he snuffed out his rushlight with his fingers. He passed through an archway into a long corridor lit by flaming torches. Cells encased in iron bars lined one side of the walls. The door to one stood open, the others empty. To the right of them, a flight of stairs snaked away up into the heart of the abbey.

Damian retreated out of sight around the corner, where he settled down to wait. An hour passed, making him curse under his breath. They had to leave before daylight. Where was Crow?

At the crunch of heavy boots on the stairs, Damian stood, ready for flight. Soldiers' voices, jesting and laughing, echoed throughout the dungeon. He chanced a quick look. Two guards dragged a limp man down the stairs. A big, beefy fellow followed, who must have been the turnkey. They hauled the semiconscious man through the cell door and threw him roughly down. The door clanged shut. The turnkey hastened forward. A key rasped as it turned in the lock. Then the three climbed the stairs.

Damian emerged and ran over to stare into the stinking cell. The fair-haired man lay where they'd left him, eyes closed. Was he Halcrow? Damian gripped the bars of the door and rattled it. It didn't budge, and there was no key in the lock. "Crow?" he murmured softly.

In the flickering light, the man raised his head. Foggy-blue eyes stared at him. "Am I dreaming? Can it be you, Beau?"

Damian nodded with relief. "'Tis I. Here to get you out."

Crow chuckled weakly. "How do you propose to do that? The French are here in great numbers. Eager to see a hanging. It's set for tomorrow at sunrise."

"Then they're doomed to disappointment."

He straightened his back and groaned. "Save yourself, Beau. Go now. Before they discover you."

"I need to open the cell door. Where do they keep the key? Does the turnkey carry it?"

"On his belt. Big bruiser, he is, too. Sits in that chair down at the end of the corridor. He'll be back soon. Snores like the very devil, along with other disgusting habits."

Clomping boots sounded on the stairs. "Might have to disappear for a bit. Get ready to run."

Crow chuckled again. "I'd like to oblige you, good fellow."

"No bones broken?"

"No, but I'm at least an inch taller."

Wondering if Giles could stand, let alone run, after enduring the rack, Damian slipped back out of sight and waited, hunkered down in a dark corner. The jailer's heavy footfalls filled the chamber, then a scrape and a protesting groan from the chair as he sat on it. Damian attempted to calculate how many hours of darkness they had left. At a guess, two, or three at the most. They had to leave soon, or Pole might not wait. He urged himself to be patient, pulling his knees up and wrapping his arms around them, the chill of the stone floor seeping into his bones.

Minutes passed and turned into twenty. Then, heavy snores,

loud enough to rattle the rafters, filled the chamber. Damian risked a look. The big fellow slumped in his chair, with his brawny arms hanging loosely at his sides. He had propped up a rifle against the wall beside him, and an empty bottle of wine lay on its side on the floor. Snorts and wheezes emitted from the turnkey's thick lips, the big, rusty key hanging invitingly from the belt around his big belly.

Damian pulled the knife from his boot and crept toward the sleeping man. Crow had moved close to the door and was gingerly stretching out his legs. He raised a fist, urging Damian on.

Glad to find Crow ambulant at least, Damian gripped the knife, aware of the need to silence this brute swiftly—before the mob heard him and swarmed down the stairs.

The man's bloodshot eyes flew open, his hand grasping for his rifle. He opened his mouth to yell. Damian punched him hard in his soft stomach. The guard grunted and the air hissed through his lips, but his strength proved as strong as a bull as he grappled with Damian for the knife. Struggling to his feet, he came at Damian, but the wine had made him clumsy. Damian slipped a foot behind the man's knee and pushed him off his feet, finishing the move with a fast slash to his thick neck. Then Damian bent and grabbed the key from the man's belt and ran over to the cell.

"Neatly done," came a fierce whisper from Crow. The door unlocked, Damian supported him, an arm around his shoulders, and they hastened to the storeroom as voices sounded somewhere above them, growing louder.

Damian eased Crow into the small space and shut the door behind them. He shifted to open the other door into pitch dark. The rushlight had crumpled to dust. "Careful," he whispered. "There are five steps down."

They descended with more caution than Damian would have liked. Finally, they found themselves out in the graveyard, dragging in lungfuls of fresh air. Damian cursed as the dawn arrived with a showy display in the east. They had no choice but to make their escape in daylight.

"We are to ride that nag?" Crow viewed the horse with dismay.

"The best I could do. Don't insult Lucifer. He's all we have."

"And glad of him," Crow hastily amended, giving the horse's neck a pat.

It was a painfully slow journey back along the road. Lucifer, with a belly full of grass, plodded along, unfazed by the men's urging. Damian kept glancing behind him, expecting to see the guards riding toward them, but so far, they'd been lucky. Men would soon be sent out to scour the roads after searching the abbey.

Pole, as good as his word, waited with the trap by the willows. "I wouldn't have believed it, if I hadn't seen it with my own eyes," he said. "I'd like to hear how you managed it."

"Happy to oblige once we're away." Damian gave Crow a leg up onto the trap. They still had miles to go. It would be a nerve-wracking journey until they reached the safety of the Channel waters.

⇶✦⇷

POLE AND HIS companions melted away like smoke, minutes before de Marmont's men rode onto the beach, rifles poised. They pointlessly fired over the water as the fishing boat carrying Halcrow and Damian set sail for England.

On deck, Halcrow leaned back against a basket of nets. "I can't believe I'm on my way home. Never thought I'd see it again."

Damian perched on an upturned drum. Seagulls filled the sky, calling in the hope of a fish feed, then swooping down to the dark-gray, choppy water. He shaded his eyes. "I can see the outline of the English coast. Won't be long now."

"I am in your debt, Ballantine," Halcrow said, dispensing with their aliases. "Have I told you how appreciative I am?"

"You have, several times. And I have told you, several times, it is unnecessary. It goes with the job."

"The job, yes." Halcrow looked thoughtful as he pushed his blond hair out of his eyes. He was in much better shape than Damian had feared. "Which I don't wish to be a part of anymore."

"You will feel like that for a while," Damian said. "But it will draw you in again."

"No. I'm finished. My beautiful bride, whom I haven't yet bedded, waits for me."

"I'm sure you'll make up for lost time." Damian laughed, but it surprised him. A married spy? He rarely came across it.

"My estate needs me," Halcrow said. "I intend to spend my days there with my wife, fill my nursery, and raise sheep. But first I must see what Scovell has in mind for me."

"I wish you well with that." Damian watched as they approached the coast of east Kent. They'd dock before nightfall. Halcrow had made him evaluate what he wanted for himself. When he reached Longview Hall two days hence, he'd make plans. For the first time since he'd begun his mission, he allowed himself to think about Diana. Her lovely face swept into his mind's eye. How passionate and curious a lover she would be. He wanted her for himself, but it may not be possible. With her father eager to have her married, there could already be another man in her life. He frowned, not wanting to travel down that road. But despite his reluctance, he had to face the truth. He loved her. A feeling strange to him. Glorious, but fraught with possible heartbreak. He'd never been in love before. While he'd cared for past lovers, this urge to be with one woman night and day was new to him. He'd never felt the urge to stake his claim on any woman as he did now. His and Diana's experience in the carriage had left him shaken. He'd wanted so much more, and so had she. Had he let her slip through his fingers? He'd been a fool. But that was with the benefit of hindsight. He might have died back there in France. The wind caught his soft moan and carried it away. But Halcrow stared at him, noting his expression.

"There's a lady in your life too, my friend. If you care for her, don't lose her. Not to this business. Wellesley will win this war, no matter what we choose to do."

⟫⟫✕⟪⟪

HALCROW'S WORDS LINGERED when Damian, weary to his bones, entered his house two days later and handed his hat, coat, and gloves to the butler. "Pay the jarvie, will you, Barron?"

"Good to have you home, my lord."

Max scampered into the hall with a woof of welcome, his feathery tail wagging madly. Damian rubbed the dog's silky ears and permitted a lick on his face before he edged the dog away. "Good to see you, fellow."

Luke hurried in. "Thank heaven." He shrugged sheepishly. "I must admit to feeling great relief to see you in one piece."

Damian accepted it was worse for Luke, who had to wait for news, than it was for him amid the action. They walked to the library, where he intended to enjoy a glass of their best claret before going up to bathe and change. "Any news?" he asked once he'd folded himself into his chair and taken up the glass of wine.

Luke's eyes looked bright and purposeful. Something Damian had not seen in a long time. "Rather a lot."

"Don't keep me guessing."

"It concerns a lady," Luke said, looking abashed. "I think you'll approve of Miss Emily Brentwood. She is quite charming."

Damian chuckled and leaned back against the highbacked wingchair, putting his feet on the ottoman. "I imagine she is."

"I've begun work on my house. It should be ready for occupation within a couple of months."

"Well, fancy." Damian grinned. "That is excellent news. Does this mean you're contemplating marrying the lady?"

Luke nodded. "I hope to. Haven't asked her yet. I trust this won't make things difficult for you."

"Actually, it fits in nicely with my plans."

Luke looked intrigued. "Which are?"

"To return here and run the estate. No more adventures. At least not those on the high seas."

With a sigh, his brother raked his hands through his hair. "That eases my mind." He raised a dark eyebrow. "I imagine a lady has something to do with this decision?"

Damian frowned. "Maybe. I hope so. It's complicated."

"Best not dally, then, brother." Luke suddenly stood. "I forgot! A letter came for you from a Lady Diana Stafford."

Damian was on his feet. "What? Where is it?"

Luke, already at the desk, sifted through papers. He located it and handed it to him. "I hope you don't mind, but I thought it best to open it. And I replied to Lady Diana to say you were away."

Damian studied it, reading between the lines of Diana's polite words with growing concern. She would not have written after the words exchanged at their parting unless she had been desperate. Lord Montgomery had asked for her hand and her father had accepted him. She hoped to learn something about the viscount that would cause her father to refuse him.

He was already at the door when he turned and spoke to his surprised brother. "I must go to London. I need to see Scovell."

"What, tonight?" Luke asked, following him out. "At least have a bite of supper first."

Chapter Twenty

DIANA SAT IN the morning room, gazing at the announcement of their engagement in *The Morning Post*, which also appeared in *The Morning Herald*, *The Times*, and *The Morning Chronical*. She pushed the newspaper away despondently as her grandmother came in holding a letter.

Diana sat up. "Is it from Lady Slade?"

"Yes." With a rustle of perfumed violet taffeta, which suited her silver hair, the dowager duchess joined Diana on the sofa. "Lady Slade writes that Lord Montgomery proposed to her daughter, Felicity, some time ago. She and Slade were pleased at first, as he was very presentable, with excellent manners and an income of six thousand a year. But when Felicity told them he'd expressed strong views about Bonaparte, whom he confessed to greatly admire, they decided it was best to refuse him." Grandmama folded the letter. "Slade is a staunch royalist."

Diana sighed. "That's not enough, is it? Papa might already know of this. Other friends of his express similar views."

"Yes, the Hollands make no secret of it," Grandmama said with a grimace. "I'm sorry, my dear."

Diana picked up a sofa cushion and twirled the fringe through her fingers while she tested the idea she'd formed during the previous sleepless night. "Grandmama, perhaps you could invite Lord Montgomery to dine here with Papa? I can invite Lord

Montgomery to stroll with me in the garden and prod him to speak his mind about his opinion of me, and what a wife should be, while you maneuver Papa onto the balcony, where he can overhear us."

Grandmama looked skeptical. "I could never *maneuver* your father anywhere, even when he was a little boy. But I'll endeavor to try."

"Good," Diana said, with a lift of her spirits. "But it must be soon."

"I must consult your father's secretary. We'll arrange dinner here for an evening when he isn't otherwise engaged. I'll tell him I wish to talk to Lord Montgomery before the wedding."

"Perfect!" Diana jumped up. "Tims must launder my prettiest gown."

"I never thought to see you employ feminine wiles, Diana," Grandmama said with a chuckle.

"I'm willing to do almost anything," Diana murmured as she exited the room. It would shock her grandmother to learn just how far she would go.

Papa and Lord Montgomery attended Grandmama's dinner the following evening. Delicious food and the best wines were served, and the meal seemed a pleasant affair, with Lord Montgomery at his most charming, which Diana always distrusted.

When the men joined them in the drawing room after their port, Diana invited Montgomery to stroll in the garden.

"A delightful idea," he said after a quick study of her face.

"Yes, indeed. It is such a fine evening, is it not?" Grandmama put a hand on her father's shoulder as he went to rise from his chair. "Shall we allow the couple to have a moment alone, Frederick?"

"Very well." He looked resigned but settled back in his chair.

The rear garden was not large, but it was well-designed to create interesting spaces to wander about in. Hedges framed a small fountain where water flowed from a Grecian maiden's urn into a pool, hiding the terrace from view.

Diana's nerves were raw. "How do you feel the war is progressing, Lord Montgomery?" she asked, her shaky voice betraying her.

"Let us not talk about war on a night like this." He stepped closer and gazed down at her, his expression unreadable in the flickering light of a brazier. "Dare I hope you have softened your view of marriage, Lady Diana? And of me?"

She stepped back closer to the hedge. "I hoped you might have changed your views," she said. "You said that you would treat me like your…"

Lord Montgomery moved close again, and his hands bit hard into her shoulders while he forced his mouth against hers to stifle any chance at speech. She felt a sharp pain on her breast. Diana, shocked, wriggled back to elude him. But he held her fast while whispering in her ear. "I shan't fall for your tricks, Lady Diana. I urge you to behave yourself or you will suffer the consequences once you become Lady Montgomery."

Diana struggled free and hurried around the hedge. But the terrace where she'd expected to find Papa was empty.

Diana saw concern in Grandmama's eyes when she entered the drawing room. Flustered, her face hot, she could say or do nothing to criticize Lord Montgomery, who, looking jovial, fulsomely praised the gardens.

After a game of whist, her father and Lord Montgomery departed into the night, leaving Diana to explain what had occurred. "Lord Montgomery guessed what I was about. He kissed me to quieten me. It was horrible." She scrubbed her mouth again with her handkerchief and shuddered. "Papa didn't hear any of it, did he?"

Grandmama shook her head, looking rueful. "Your father complained it was too cool and retreated inside. Other than tackling him, I could do nothing." She paused. "Next time, I could trip up Lord Montgomery. I should have better success with that."

Diana giggled. "We'll just have to think up another strategy, Grandmama." She stared into space. "Perhaps I could run away." She knew trying to escape was futile, but she must act!

"Over my dead body," Grandmama said forcefully. "And you must promise me when God takes me, you will *never* consider doing such a thing. Running away is cowardly. There are ways to make a life for yourself, even within a marriage."

Grandmama was trying to console her, but she only made her feel worse. Diana sighed. "I suppose so, Grandmama." She trudged up the stairs, trying not to think of Lord Montgomery's forceful, revolting mouth on hers and how he'd taken the opportunity to pinch her hard on the breast.

⤜⤛⟪⟫⤚⤝

DAMIAN LEFT HIS Mayfair house after breakfast the next morning, having managed only two hours of sleep. During the journey back to London, he'd felt raw but grimly determined. He would swear Montgomery was more than just a French sympathizer; he was a spy involved in stealing specific information relating to Wellesley's next campaign. And the only Englishman he'd seen out in the garden that night had been Montgomery. As well as the Frenchman Charles Moreau, who had apparently gone missing since, he'd been informed by Scovell. It became imperative that Damian find that proof and hopefully locate the other missing document.

Scovell was already at his desk in his office at Horse Guards. He looked up from writing when Damian entered. "A mission well accomplished, Ballantine! I received a glowing report from Halcrow." He put down his quill and gestured to a chair with a warm smile. "You are due for a well-earned rest."

"Not until I've got Montgomery." Damian sat back and crossed his legs. "Have your men discovered anything?"

His spymaster raised his eyebrows. "I gather you haven't seen the newspapers?"

Damian shook his head. "Not yet. Why?"

"Lord Montgomery and Lady Diana Stafford's wedding is to take place at the duke's estate in a sennight."

Damian cursed under his breath. "What unseemly haste. What does Montgomery fear?"

Scovell's intelligent eyes studied Damian's face. "A surprising overreaction. You have more than a casual interest in the lady?"

"Is Montgomery still followed?"

Scovell shook his head. "He's about to marry a duke's daughter. We can't pursue it until we have proof. And we are short of men. They have far more important tasks to occupy them."

"Then I shall take it over." *Montgomery will consider himself safe now. He might grow careless.*

"If you wish. It is on your own time, after all."

Damian stood, fighting frustration and anger. "And if I discover he carries his affection for Bonaparte further than any decent Englishman should?"

"I doubt he'd have that document. He'd have passed it on like a hot potato, unless something has held things up. Moreau has made himself scarce, so it's possible he was meant to be the courier. If you find Montgomery is involved, deal with him," Scovell said bluntly. "But be discreet. I don't want to hear about it until I read it in the newspapers."

Damian began his pursuit of Montgomery by first visiting his club, Brooks's, on St. James's Street. He spoke to a waiter whom he'd paid for information in the past and discovered that every night Montgomery spent at the club dining and gambling, he always left at ten o'clock.

"Perhaps a lady, my lord?" the waiter ventured, tucking the coin into his coat pocket.

"Some intrigue, I imagine," Damian replied, impatient to find something concrete to use against Montgomery while troubled by how little time he had to act. While he fervently wished to see Diana and assure her she wasn't alone, he couldn't. He was unable to take any action until he had proof.

The following evening, Montgomery visited the club.

Damian waited in a hackney. Sure enough, at ten o'clock, Montgomery left the club and hailed a carriage. He might have had a mistress, but Damian doubted the man would be so punctual. He followed Montgomery's hackney at a discreet distance as they wound their way through the dirty and dangerous streets of St. Giles.

At the apex of the Seven Dials, the hackney pulled up outside the Red Cow. Montgomery alighted, paid the jarvie, and disappeared inside the pub.

Crossing the pavement, Damian gazed through the dirty windows in time to see Montgomery climb the stairs.

A mistress in the Red Cow wasn't entirely impossible. The man was capable of anything, but Damian doubted it would be a woman Montgomery sought. He wouldn't want to risk getting the pox, not when his money could buy him any high-class courtesan in London he fancied. But who knew the tastes of such men?

Damian went through the door into the crowded, smoky pub, noting the smells of hops, sour bodies, and a distinct aura of despair. The patrons hovered over their tables, intent on drinking themselves to oblivion or arguing among themselves. No one bothered to look his way as he took the stairs.

At the top, three doors opened onto a small landing. He listened at one and heard only the groans of its inhabitants. The sound of snoring boomed out from behind another. Muffled voices came from the next. Two men, by the sound of it. His heart took a leap when he heard a Frenchman speak and Montgomery answer.

Damian drew his pistol from beneath his coat. He raised his foot and kicked the thin, wooden door open. It flew back with a resounding bang and hung off its hinges. Its two occupants stared at him, stunned. In front of them on the table was a large document.

The Frenchman started to rise. *"Mon Dieu!"*

"Remain seated, if you wish to live." Damian kept his pistol aimed at Montgomery.

The Frenchman, a swarthy fellow with angry, brown eyes, shifted in his chair.

"Don't move, you fool," Montgomery cried. "He will shoot me first."

Unwilling to wait, the Frenchman dived for the gun inside his coat. Damian fired, and a bloom of red spread out over his coat. He fell back with a gurgle and rolled off the chair to the floor.

Montgomery barely glanced at him. His hard eyes watched Damian with furious spite. "Such violence, Ballantine. Surely, it's unnecessary? We are reasonable men. I have important friends you will anger should you murder an unarmed lord in cold blood."

"I don't intend for them to find out." With an eye on Montgomery, Damian moved over to the document. It was the one of Scovell's meant for the diplomatic pouch thought to be stolen at the same time as the other. Their courier had never left England; he'd been found near the docks with his throat cut. Damian backed up and gestured with his pistol. "Let's go somewhere quiet to discuss it." It was always possible one of the more sober drinkers below might mount the stairs, roused by the gunshot. That would confuse matters. "Keep your hands where I can see them."

Montgomery rose slowly from the table and raised his hands. "You have one ball left in that pistol. What happens if you miss me?"

"I never miss."

Damian snatched up the document and slipped it inside his coat. They left the room and descended to where a bleary-eyed audience made no move to stop them. Damian poked Montgomery in the back and they walked out into the street. He gestured around the corner. They stepped into an alley poorly lit by candlelight from the pub windows. "You won't kill me. It's hardly the act of one gentleman to another," Montgomery said.

"Would you prefer to hang as a traitor?" Damian prodded him farther into the shadows.

"Don't you want to know why?" he asked, stalling for time.

"Not particularly. People like you, who would sell out your own country, shouldn't be given a voice."

Montgomery sneered. "Nothing you or any of your misguided patriots try to do will beat Bonaparte. He is a tactician par excellence. The world has never seen the like."

"And hopefully never will again," Damian said grittily.

Montgomery stumbled. As he went down on one knee to steady himself, a small gun appeared in his hand from a holster strapped to his ankle. He whirled on Damian, his finger already on the trigger.

His shot went wide, biting off a piece of brick on the wall, but Damian's ball found its mark on Montgomery's chest.

Montgomery, surprise in his eyes, crumpled on the ground, his face taking on a blueish tinge. Spread-eagled on the pavement, blood seeping from his white cravat, he fought to speak.

Damian knelt beside him, expecting some last request. "What is it?"

"England will lose the war, you fools." His head fell back.

Damian straightened. He tucked his pistol back into his breeches, put two fingers to his mouth, and whistled.

A small carriage lumbered around the corner. Two men jumped down. "Feed him to the fishes, guv?" one of them politely inquired as they levered Montgomery up into it.

"Yes. Empty his wallet, but leave any identification, if you will. There's another body upstairs in the pub." He drew the heavy sack of coins from his pocket and handed it to the man.

"Thanks, guv."

Damian left them and strolled back into the main thoroughfare in search of a hackney. He was satisfied with the night's work. Scovell might not be prepared to go public with it, but he would be relieved.

Chapter Twenty-One

DIANA GAZED IN the mirror with a groan. A purple bruise on her breast would mean wearing a fichu with her favorite gown. Why should she care? She did not wish to dress to please Lord Montgomery, who had spitefully caused the mark. Her breath caught. The wedding was in three days' time. It kept her awake at night, which made her skin too pale. There were dark circles under her eyes.

At breakfast, Papa commented on her appearance. He attacked his bacon and eggs while telling her that most brides were nervous before their weddings.

She chewed her lip, fearing she would say something to anger him. It was too late. Her wedding gown was ready, her trousseau packed. Several hundred guests would fill the chapel as, according to Billings, her father's secretary, everyone had accepted the invitation.

Papa took up his knife and fork. "I expected a word from Montgomery before this. The reverend waits to be advised as to how many of Montgomery's guests would attend, and we are yet to find out who is to be his best man. My secretary wrote to remind the viscount but tells me his letter has gone unanswered."

"Perhaps he is away in the country." *Or he changed his mind and fled England,* she thought hopefully.

"He might be seeing to changes to his country estate. Ensuring it is perfect for you, my dear."

Diana put down her toast, which threatened to choke her. She doubted Lord Montgomery would bother to please her. Whatever he thought of her, it was closer to dislike than love. And despite that, he was determined to marry her.

Ballantine hadn't replied to her letter, either. Now that she'd left London, she didn't know if he'd returned from overseas. Was he all right? It tormented her to think he might not have been. He had to have been alive and happy, somewhere in the world, even if he wasn't with her.

"I'll go for my ride," she said, rising from the table.

"It's always been my intention to see you happy, Diana," Papa said as she went to the door. "I promised your mother before she left us to find a good man for you."

Diana's shoulders sagged. She wanted to say, "*That good man is not Lord Montgomery,*" but she resisted as he looked more upset than she'd ever seen him. She bent over him at his chair and gave him a quick kiss. Papa patted her cheek. "Enjoy your ride. And take the groom," he called after her.

At the stables, Diana mounted Artemis and rode out with Peter following. She now loathed the man and didn't trust him. She made a concerted effort to lose him, which was easy with her superior horse. When she returned from a fast ride over the fields, to tire herself, she hoped she could sleep tonight. Speirs met her in the hall and informed her of her father's wish to see her in his study.

Papa looked up from his desk with a grave expression. "I have received a letter from Lord Montgomery's secretary. He has been missing for several days, ever since he visited his club. It is most uncharacteristic of him. He didn't attend his appointment with his tailor for the last fitting of his wedding clothes. They hold grave fears for him."

Diana's heart leaped. He had fled the country! She'd always suspected he was a spy for the French.

The next two days passed without a word of Lord Montgomery's whereabouts. The wedding preparations came to a halt. Diana spent most of the day with her grandmother in the dower house. She prayed that he had changed his mind, but she feared that her hopes would be dashed again if he suddenly contacted them. Would her father forgive him for disappearing without a word and causing the wedding to be canceled? He just might, as he'd changed his mind about Montgomery once before.

"I'll take Artemis out for some exercise, Grandmama," she said, so restless, she was sick of herself and feared she worried her grandmother.

Diana took her daily route along the boundary between her father's estate and the road. She liked to visit the place where Ballantine's coach had been held up. It brought him sharply to mind. But it was foolish to go on visiting the spot. With a soft moan, she was about to turn Artemis's head for home when a man shouted her name from beyond the hedge.

It wasn't... It couldn't have been? But that deep voice could only belong to one man. She rode to the break in the hedge and pushed through.

A coach waited beside the road. A gentleman, his hat pulled low, watched her ride toward him. Those shoulders, those long legs... She gasped, dismounted, dropping the reins, and ran to him. *Ballantine!* Her voice caught in her throat, blocked by a rush of hot tears. She threw herself onto his chest and into his arms.

"Hey." He caught her and, laughing, swung her around. "That is quite a welcome."

She reached up and touched his dear face. "I didn't know if you were...alive."

"Do I not seem so?"

She punched him lightly on the chest. "You might have answered my letter. To stop me from worrying about you."

A smile raised his lips. "I thought it better not to, sweetheart."

"Ballantine, Lord Montgomery is missing. The wedding was to be held on Saturday, but now..."

"I know." He picked up Artemis's reins before the mare could stir up the carriage horses and threw them over a bush. Then, taking Diana's hand, he led her into the trees. Screened from view, he turned to her. "They found his body in the Thames."

"Oh!"

"Do you mind very much?" His serious, brown eyes searched hers.

"I loathed him. Is it horrid of me to be glad he's gone from my life? I am sure he spied for the French."

"He wasn't a good man, sweetheart."

She wondered briefly if Ballantine knew more about it, and if he would ever tell her. "Have you come to advise my father of his death?"

"He will have heard it by now. I encountered the magistrate on his way to call on him."

"You came to see me?" She held her breath.

"I needed to see you first. I know of your preference to go out early. I hoped you'd ride this way again. If not, I would have come tomorrow on horseback. Rode over the estate until I found you. I'll call on your father, but coming so soon after Montgomery's death, now is not the right time." He swept off his hat and wrapped his arms around her, his eyes darkening with emotion. "Diana, I want nothing more than to share my life with you. I no longer work for the government. I love you. I adore you. I simply can't live without you. Will you marry me?"

"Yes, oh, yes," she said. His familiar smell enveloped her, stirring her to passion. She reached up and pushed a lock of his disordered, dark-brown hair back from his broad forehead. "I love you with all my heart and soul, Ballantine. I would marry you tomorrow."

He kissed her. His lips softened against hers, his tongue seeking hers. She opened her mouth for him, and her knees sagged, her head swimming while her heart pounded with joy. His muscular arms brought their coach ride to mind. Every cherished detail to which she'd clung while her hopes and dreams had died, and her future had looked bleak and without love.

Ballantine drew away. "This is what we must do. After a reasonable period, ask your father if you may return to London for the last few weeks of summer. Many of the *ton* will still be in the city, at least until the shooting season begins in autumn. I'm sure he will be happy to oblige you. I'll court you in the proper manner before asking the duke for your hand."

Diana stared at him, dismayed. "But that will take weeks or more! Can we not elope?"

He shook his head. "No, my love."

She recognized that resolute look. Ballantine was, at least in matters concerning her, a conventional man, and very protective of her. It would be impossible to change his mind. "How disappointing," she couldn't help saying.

He raised her chin with his finger and smiled into her eyes. "It would cause an uproar, Diana. I refuse to subject you to vicious gossip. We must do this properly." His gaze implored her. "We have the rest of our lives to be together."

She sighed and ran her hand regretfully over his waistcoat of gray-and-burgundy-striped silk, and his hard chest beneath. "Very well, Damian."

He took her hand and led her back to Artemis. With another quick kiss, he assisted her to mount. She sat on her horse, watching as he leaped into the coach. He blew her a kiss through the window. The coachman urged the horses on, and the fine carriage raced away along the road.

In a matter of a bare few minutes, her life had changed forever. She laughed and leaned over to stroke her horse's silky flank. "Am I not the luckiest girl in the world, Artemis?"

⤜≫≪⤛

BEFORE GOING TO see Diana, Damian had handed the stolen dispatch over to Scovell.

"Excellent. Did you intend Montgomery's body to be found?"

Scovell asked, casting an eye over the document before putting it down.

"No. But it puts an end to the mystery of his disappearance. There will always be speculation as to how and why he died."

"Yes, but it will die down after a time. There's always something else to distract the public. What are your plans?"

"I intend to marry Lady Diana Stafford. I'll live a quiet life from now on."

Scovell arched an eyebrow. "Ah." He leaned back in his chair. "Are you sure you can give up this life? Many find it difficult."

"Very sure."

"There are others in this spy ring we must find. I'm disappointed you won't be in on the chase. As will Wellesley be. You're one of the best." He smiled. "I hope to receive an invitation to the wedding."

"I'm not sure when it will be, but I'd be delighted to see you there, sir."

Scovell rose and came around his desk. He offered his hand, and Damian shook it. "My very best to you and your bride-to-be."

"Thank you."

Donning his hat, Damian left Horse Guards. It was a perfect late summer day. The green leaves on the trees in the avenue were stirred by a fresh wind. Life had taken quite a turn. And he was more than ready for it.

Epilogue

Longview Hall, Berkshire, November

T HE MOON SHONE in through the break in the curtains. Beneath the soft candlelight of the chandelier in the earl's bedchamber, Damian shed his clothes while Diana watched him. She craved him, savored every part of him. He was beautiful, like a Greek god one found in marble statues, with his strongly muscled shoulders and broad torso tapering to a slim waist, narrow hips and long, powerful legs. She curled her fingers into her palms, wanting to trail them over his smooth, warm skin, to trace the contours of the bones, sinews, and muscles, and feel the rasp of dark chest hair, which narrowed down beneath the waist of his pantaloons.

He undid the buttons and stepped out of them. She caught her breath at his already burgeoning erection. Trembling, she tucked her hands between her thighs, where the damp heat of her own body already throbbed with intense desire.

Seated on the bedroom chair, he stripped off his stockings.

Penny had been her bridesmaid—Diana had been too sad to ask her when she'd expected to marry Montgomery—and Damian's brother, Luke, had served as the best man at their wedding ceremony held in London at St. Georges. Her father's mansion in Grosvenor Square had hosted the reception. She thought her father had looked relieved when she'd said goodbye before leaving with Damian for Longview Hall, but he'd had a charming lady he'd been courting for the past month on his arm, so perhaps he wouldn't be lonely in that big house.

She and Damian could not decide where to spend their honeymoon, in the end deciding they just wanted to be together at home. When the war ended, he promised to take her to Paris.

They spent the following days and nights loving each other, in bed and out, until they were claimed by exhausted sleep. She loved to wake and find him beside her. It stirred her passion all over again and rivaled his. According to Damian, they were a match made in heaven.

This morning, they rode out as usual after breakfast through the woods to the river and beyond. She admired his strong, well-shaped hands, steady on the reins, remembering how magical they could be on her skin, and laughed when his big, enthusiastic, and rather beautiful dog, Max, raced along behind them.

Damian had taken her again, leaning back against a sturdy oak. The loud rush of the river in her ears failed to drown out her cries as his hands cupped on her bottom and raised her to meet his thrusts and she coiled her legs around his waist.

Afterward, she giggled weakly and confessed to being unable to find the energy to ride home. "Perhaps we can live here in the forest and eat berries," she suggested.

"Berries? I need a steak. And I prefer our bed at night, with you beside me, and preferably under me, my love."

She flushed at his bold language. But she loved it. Loved everything about him. This was what she had always known she wanted deep down but had never expected to have. A husband who truly loved her, who desired her, and knew how to satisfy her.

She pushed the thoughts away as Damian walked naked over to the bed. "Why are you wearing this?" He bent over her, fingering the froth of lace at her breast. "The nightgown is beautiful, but you're more beautiful without it."

With one swift motion, he pulled the delicate fabric over her head and tossed it onto a chair.

She gasped. "Nuns in Belgium made that lace. It cost Papa a fortune."

"Made with passionate frustration, I imagine. I shall buy you more. You can wear them when our hair turns gray, and we are afflicted with rheumatism. Until then, we sleep naked."

The heat in his chocolate-brown eyes thrilled her, heavy lidded with amorous intent. He joined her on the bed, easing her closer, burrowing his face into her long tresses.

"I love the sweet smell of your hair," he murmured, his warm, wine-scented breath on her neck. "And the taste of you." When he kissed her passionately, her breath caught, then he pressed his lips to the pulse in her throat. Shaping her breasts in his hands, he bent to lick a nipple, circling it gently with a finger, then caught it in his teeth and suckled. Diana moaned. When the nipple became sensitive and hard, he moved to the other one.

His hand swept up her thigh, settling between her legs. He thumbed her sensitive bud and slipped a finger inside her. She writhed helplessly as her body coiled, sending her into paroxysms of exquisite pleasure.

"Come for me, darling."

She murmured some inarticulate reply as a heightened feeling, friction, and craving built within her.

DAMIAN'S BREATH EXPELLED from his lips as Diana took him in her hand and fondled him. She was beautiful, this extraordinary wife of his. That he might have lost her made him catch his breath, even now. She was so precious, it sometimes made him fearful. What if she became pregnant? Women suffered a great deal in childbirth. But all thoughts faded as she slid her hands up and down his cock and fondled the hooded head. Diana was an instinctive lover. She already knew just how to please him. Loving her was different each time. She could always surprise him. If God granted them a long life, he would never grow tired of being with her, loving her.

He groaned and placed his hand over hers before the building sensation became too much to bear. "Best not, my love."

Damian took control again before it ended there. He framed her face with his hands and his mouth covered hers with a deep kiss, their tongues meeting in a sensual dance. He drew away and, parting her legs, moved over her, breathing in the womanly scent of her arousal. Then he entered her with a swift push and a moan of pleasure.

They moved as one, his thrusts slow and deliberate, while he savored every sensation, every kiss, every cry of pleasure from her lips.

THE FEELING, THE friction, increased in rhythmic time as he pushed deeper. Diana raised her legs around his hips, holding him tightly, feeling the rasp of his chest hair against her breasts. His thrusts quickened. Their panting breaths filled the room, and a tightening in her belly heralded another climax. It soon carried her away.

Feeling deliciously languid, her knees flopped wide, and she moaned, loving the loud growl Damian made as he came. For a moment, he stilled, his panting breath stirring her hair, and then he rolled away to gather her close beside him.

Diana rested a leg over his stomach, sated and sleepy.

His hand stroked the length of her calf.

"Damian?"

"Mm?"

"Tomorrow, shall we ride over and visit Luke? See how he's faring? He will be sad now that Miss Brentwood has become engaged to another man." She frowned. "How awful of her father to insist she marry the baron when she and Luke loved each other. Fathers can be so ruthless with their daughters."

"My brother can perfectly handle his own romances, my love. Without our interference."

She rolled over on top of him, her breasts flattening against his chest. Aware of the flare of desire in his eyes, she smiled. "I rather thought we could invite Penny to stay? She is in the doldrums after the man she hoped to marry failed to come up to scratch. I believe she and Luke would like each other."

"Hush." He lightly smacked her bottom, then circled it with his palm, rubbing it better. "A man needs his sleep if he's to keep his woman satisfied." He reached over and snuffed out the candle.

Diana giggled and nestled into his side. Her head against his chest, she closed her eyes.

⟫⟩⟨⟪

RETURNING FROM BREAKFAST, Diana met the butler in the hall.

"A letter has arrived for you, my lady."

"Thank you, Barron." Surprised, she turned the slim missive over in her hands as she went upstairs. At her desk, she took out the mother-of-pearl letter opener and slit it open.

It was a bare few lines. *We have a daughter! We've called her Diana. I wish the same for you, dearest. A long, happy life with your love!* There were several kisses but no signature. Diana lowered the letter and sobbed. Anne had a daughter.

Damian came in and found her wiping her eyes with her handkerchief.

"What is it, my love?" he asked with concern.

She handed him the letter, and with a frown, he read it. He glanced up. "It's from Lady Anne?"

Diana nodded. "I thought never to hear from her. Perhaps we could visit her again sometime? I know she was worried about her secret being divulged, but you already know about her, and we're skilled at traveling discreetly. When we can trust the groom," she added, still annoyed with Peter. "I shall write and ask her."

Damian drew her up and wrapped his arms around her, his hand on the back of her hair. "It is good to hear from her, yes?"

She nodded again and sobbed against his chest.

He raised her chin and kissed her lips. "There are certain things about women I will never understand. A man would be happy for good news," he murmured against her hair. "Then he would put the letter away in a drawer, his cheeks perfectly dry."

"Men." She pushed him away with a laugh.

Dear readers,

There are real-life characters in this book, but it is a work of fiction. I have taken license with them and the times they lived in to fit my story. Lord Holland and Lady Holland were real people. Holland House in Kensington still stands. And it was true that the baron and his wife were devotees of Bonaparte.

I hope you enjoy my book.

Maggi

About the Author

A USA TODAY bestselling author of Regency romances, with over 35 books published, Maggi's Regency series are International bestsellers. Stay tuned for Maggi's latest Regency series out next year. Her novels include Victorian mysteries, contemporary romantic suspense and young adult. Maggi holds a BA in English and Master of Arts Degree in Creative Writing. She supports the RSPCA and animals often feature in her books.

Like to keep abreast of my latest news? Join my newsletter.
http://bit.ly/1m70lJJ

Blog: http://bit.ly/1t7B5dx
Find excerpts and reviews on my website: http://bit.ly/1m70lJJ
Twitter: @maggiandersen: http://bit.ly/1Aq8eHg
Facebook: Maggi Andersen Author: http://on.fb.me/1KiyP9g
Goodreads: http://bit.ly/1TApe0A
Pinterest: https://www.pinterest.com.au/maggiandersen

Maggi's Amazon page for her books with Dragonblade Publishing.
https://tinyurl.com/y34dmquj